Maintaining Texas Pride

Maintaining Texas Pride

Dave Kuhne

LITERARY PRESS
LAMAR UNIVERSITY

ISBN: 978-1-942956-77-8
Library of Congress Control Number: 2020935286

Front cover: *Bridle Bit Bull* by Joe Barrington
Back cover photograph by Lynn Risser

Manufactured in the United States

Lamar University Literary Press
Beaumont, Texas

For Gordon Kuhne
brother and friend

Fiction from Lamar University Literary Press Includes

Robert Bonazzi, *Awakened by Surprise*
David Bowles, *Border Lore*
Kevin Casey, *Four Peace*
Terry Dalrymple, *Love Stories, Sort Of*
Jeffrey DeLotto, *A Caddo's Way*
Gerald Duff, *Legends of Lost Man Marsh*
Philip Gardner, *Where They Come From Where They Hide*
Andrew Geyer, *Lesser Mountains*
Britt Haraway, *Early Men*
Lynn Hoggard, *Motherland: Stories and Poems of Louisiana*
Michael Howarth, *Fair Weather Ninjas*
Gretchen Johnson, *The Joy of Deception*
Tom Mack and Andrew Geyer, editors, *A Shared Voice*
Moumin Quazi, *Migratory Words*
Harold Raley, *Lost River Anthology*
Harold Raley, *Louisiana Rogue*
Jim Sanderson, *Trashy Behavior*
Jan Seale, *Appearances*
Melvin Sterne, *The Number You Have Reached*
Melvin Sterne, *Redemption*
Melvin Sterne, *The Shoeshine Boy*
John Wegner, *Love is not a Dirty Word and Other Stories*
Robert Wexelblatt, *The Artist Wears Rough Clothing*

For more information about these and other books, go to
https://www.lamar.edu/literary-press

Acknowledgments

I would like to thank Katherine Hoerth of Lamar University Literary Press and Dan Williams of TCU Press for their insightful editorial comments and Jim Sanderson for his kind words about *Maintaining Texas Pride*. I am grateful for the friendship of encouragement of Steve Sherwood and Cynthia Shearer, my colleagues at TCU, who listened to me talk about writing this novel for at least a decade.

My sincere thanks to Joe Barrington of Red Star Studio, Throckmorton, Texas, for generously granting permission to use an image of his monumental statue, *Bridle Bit Bull*, for the cover of this book.

A version of "Magic Coins" first appeared in *Literary Fort Worth*, from TCU Press, and "The Weather and Texas Pride" was published in *Texas Weather*, an anthology from Lamar University Literary Press.

CONTENTS

Chapter 1
Tenure Review

It took only a couple of weeks for my new business to transform me from a liberal humanist to a gun toting misanthrope. It might have taken longer and the metamorphosis might have been less severe if not for the drunk and his knife that second week. The knife swinger was my introduction to being the new owner of Texas Pride self-serve coin-op car wash in Fort Worth, Texas.

I was from Fort Worth, but, as a struggling English professor at South East Panhandle State University in Grassland, Texas, I had lost touch with Cowtown, and, of course, I knew absolutely nothing about cars or car washes or machines. In fact, Dr. Collard—AKA Cowboy Tim—my department chair at SEPSU, had implied during my recent tenure evaluation that I knew nothing at all, especially about American literature or publishing academic research. I had been on shaky ground at the college ever since I was hired. Tim was a "cowboy" poet with a lisp and a black cowboy hat, and he had left my job interview early to check on contractors working on his ranch. At the time, I took that as a signal that I'd never get the position, but I later learned that Tim was the sort of academic who never let his job get in the way of his life.

Tim had published a couple of sentimental books filled with verses about horses and campfires and sunsets, and every year he was invited to read at the cowboy poetry festival that our competing university, Sul Ross State, held in Alpine. He often appeared on program at the Red Steagall Cowboy Gathering in Fort Worth, and he even read once at the national cowboy poetry conference in Nevada. In hopes of improving my chances for tenure at SEPSU, I had made it a postmodern point to privilege cowboy poetry in my American lit class, but that failed to impress either Tim or the members of my tenure committee. Tim and some of the others suspected I had an inflated sense of worth because I had taken my degree at the "big" university in Lubbock. The committee had soured on my research concerning American end-of-the-world fiction, and it soon became clear that the world *would* end before I made the SEPSU tenure cut.

When I arrived for my tenure meeting, Doris, the departmental secretary who had been pickled by a lifetime of Panhandle wind and sun, nodded me toward Tim's office without a word, a bad sign for sure. As Chair of the Department, Tim commanded the oak-paneled corner office on the second floor of the red-brick Humanities Building. The bookcases were packed with rare first editions of cowboy poetry; Tim was quite the collector, often vanishing from campus for a month at a time to do research and return with yet another obscure edition for his private library. The department rumor was that Tim's life savings and retirement were invested in the rare editions, some of which he kept in safe deposit boxes at various banks.

Tim was behind his desk, wearing his usual blue jeans, pressed white shirt, black cowboy hat and turquoise bolo. Tim's eyes were as blue and hard and cold as nuggets of gemstone. He had decorated his office with his diplomas—BA from UT Austin, MA and EdD from Texas A&I in Kingsville–and pictures of him, his wife and kids, and their horses. Smirking like a gunfighter in an old Western, Tim tipped his hat and started what I took to be a prepared speech:

"Look, Leonard. You just think this is the worst place in the world to teach, but if you don't get tenure here, you'll be lucky to get a job teaching composition at some community college. You know, the kind of place where most of the students are divorced women fleeing abuse and the major source of income in the county is welfare. I'm talking Oklahoma, boy! Anyone with any self respect would rather eat wood than do that. We better see a book soon, very soon, if you expect to stay on here."

Tim was right, of course. Most of the students at SEPSU were respectful sons and daughters of ranch owners or shop keepers or oil industry managers, not really scholars, but they were okay. I spent most of my time working with them on basic composition and providing a reading list for the rare girl who dreamed of becoming a high school English teacher. But there was no forthcoming book. There was only my one published article, the one that got me my job at SEPSU: "Gender Roles after the Collapse: Women in Contemporary American Post-Apocalyptic Fiction."

"But Tim, I published an article about women in post-apocalyptic fiction."

"Of course you did." Tim sneered. "That's the only reason we hired you three years ago. Three long years, and no progress on the book, heh?"

"I have an article: 'Literary Big Country–Just How Big Is It?' Should be out in the next issue of *Concho River Review*."

The English department at Angelo State in San Angelo

published *Concho River Review*. There was some bad blood between the SEPSU department and the Angelo State department due to a misunderstanding about committee assignments at a long forgotten South Central Modern Language Association conference. The conference had faded from memory, but the feelings lingered in an English department way.

"*Concho River Review*." Snort. "You could hide fugitives in there. You had better get writing, Leonard. The committee will need to see a book contract by the end of this semester."

But end-of-the-world fiction is depressing. Every time I started to write about McCarthy's *The Road*, I wanted to use the father's last bullet on myself. I didn't have a book; all I had was the world's worst case of writer's block. And after my meeting with Tim, I knew for certain that my days at SEPSU were numbered. So, when the authorities in Fort Worth called to tell me that Jake, my uncle on my father's side, had died, I was ready for a career change.

I was an only child, and Jake and his wife, Sue, were all of the extended family. My grandparents on both sides had passed on before Dad and Mom married, so at Christmas each year it was always just me, my folks, and Jake and Sue. And nearly every Christmas something would happen at Jake's car wash that would require his presence, and he, and sometimes Aunt Sue, would have to leave suddenly. Then, when I was in college, my folks were killed in a ferry accident while traveling in Asia. They had worked and saved for decades and had always dreamed of traveling to some exotic place. (I can still picture my mother, bless her, pouring over maps of Thailand, saying again and again, "This will be the trip of a lifetime.") Next year after that, Aunt Sue died of cancer, so there wasn't anyone for Christmas except me and Jake.

I was in grad school when he wrote me the letter and sent me the keys. For Jake, who had pretty hard bark, the note was downright sentimental. It was such a rare event to get a note from my uncle that I filed the letter (comma splices and all) along with the keys he enclosed:

Dear Leonard:

I know you and I have never done some of the things that uncles and nephews are supposed to do. We never went fishing, we never played baseball together, I never warned you about girls. But now that everyone else, Sue and your parents, are gone, and who knows how much longer I'll be around, although I'm determined to outlive my dog, Dutch, I wanted to tell you that you're a fine nephew. I was proud of you when you were a kid and I'm still proud of you now even though you're a English teacher. I'm enclosing a key to my house and a key to the equipment room at my Texas Pride car wash, just in case you need them someday. The combinations to the vaults at the car wash are written down in a book of notes I keep on my desk. I call the book Maintaining Texas Pride, in the notes are some other instructions you'll need in case you happen to find yourself responsible for the place someday. But don't worry, I'll try to sell before I give up the ghost.

Love,

Uncle Jake

At the time I laughed, not only because the notion that I might have to "maintain Texas Pride" sounded like a joke but also because Jake seemed immortal to me. Growing up and listening to my folks and Aunt Sue talk, I thought Jake was as tough as Chuck Norris, sometimes as bitter as a triple IPA, and occasionally funny or outrageous.

So I knew a little about my aunt and uncle's struggle to make a go of things in Cowtown. And I knew a little about running a business because my folks had been business people, too. My mom and dad owned an appliance sales and repair store for years. When I was in high school I worked alongside them after classes and in the summers. I suppose I was destined to be a business person, not an English professor. Besides, Pam, the grad student I'd been "advising," had finally finished her Master's degree, and she gleefully informed me (as she packed her toothpaste and her tampons) that she had taken a job in Throckmorton County, in the Texas "Big Country," teaching high school English. She was a true Texas woman, a well constructed rodeo queen with big blue eyes that always seemed to be searching the horizon.

I thought we had a strong relationship, but it obviously wasn't strong enough. We had spent two Panhandle winters hunkered down in the double bed of my double wide. Using a book of quotations and a dictionary of metaphors, we invented a game to while away the frozen nights. Whenever a substantial topic came up, we would sprinkle the conversation with some appropriate quote or allusion. For example, if the subject of my uncertain career at SEPSU and my lack of progress on the end-of-the-world book came around, Pam might chime in with a line from Thomas Carlyle: "Work is the grand cure for all the maladies and miseries." If possible, I would find a clever quote in response, like this Christopher Morley observation: "The necessity of holding a job: what an iron filing that is on the compass card of a man's brain!" We had even memorized certain quotes about certain topics, marriage for example. Pam, who had been married once, liked to cite Edith Wharton, "Marriage is not a safe anchorage but a voyage on uncharted seas." To which I would recall the line by John Gay: "No power on earth can e'er dive the knot that sacred love hath tied." I know it seems silly, but Pam and I could go on for hours playing this game.

Pam had been a scholarship barrel racer and team roper for the Tarleton Sate University rodeo team. She had a standard line about the sport: "They used to say that in barrel racing pretty girls rode fast horses, but in my experience, it was more of case of fast girls ridding pretty horses." Anyway, when she was a senior at Tarleton she suffered a tumble from her saddle and broke a leg, costing her a place on the team and her scholarship. She finished her Bachelor's in English and returned home to Perryton in the far north Panhandle. That's where her folks lived. Then there was a brief marriage that she rarely talked about to a car dealer in Amarillo. The marriage that had ended the year before Pam entered the Master's program at SEPSU. She had chosen SEPSU over Tarleton because it was hours closer to Perryton, where her family had a thousand acre ranch and where she housed her beloved horse, Tex. She considered Texas Tech but wisely decided the department was too large and chaotic for her tastes, especially since she didn't intend to go beyond the Master's. Pam and I had once made plans; now she hoped I would "understand."

What I understood as I unlocked the equipment room at my uncle's Texas Pride Car Wash just before noon that second week on the lot was that some drunk with a big knife was walking right across Berry and Cleburne and was heading straight past *Mas Ramblas* (the drive through beer barn where bikini clad *chicas* ran up to your car to take your beer order) and directly toward me. "What would Jake do?" I asked myself as the knife-welding man approached. I swung open the equipment room door, slammed it closed, and turned the heavy bolt lock. I looked through the peephole in the door to see the man, a shirtless scarecrow of rags and dirt with locks of blond hair spilling from a worn straw cowboy hat, approach the door, long knife in hand.

"Don't you go hiding from me. I know you're in there." He shook his knife and kicked the door. "Remember how you had me jailed? Well, I'm back!"

But before I could phone the police, he simply walked away. I cracked open the door and saw him stumble down the street, past Carshon's Deli, knife now holstered on his belt. Nothing I had experienced teaching American lit to ranchers' kids had prepared me for this sort of cowboy. As I watched the drunk stagger down Cleburne Road, it occurred to me that I might have been a bit too gleeful when I announced to Tim that I was resigning my position on short notice to take over my family's corporation. Of course, only I knew that I was the entire corporation, CEO and janitor, all in one package.

"You're putting the department in a tough spot, leaving without notice in mid semester. Don't expect any glowing recommendations," Tim had said.

My early departure was an inconvenience, and Tim was never one to forget or forgive an inconvenience. Inconveniences interfered with the composition of more cowboy poems. Instead of crafting verses about horses and campfires and a dead way of life, Tim would have to write an ad for the *Chronicle of Higher Education*. I could read the ad in my mind:

Wanted, young ambitious scholar who has completed the Ph. D. and looks forward to teaching three sections of composition and an American literature class each semester. Overloads and summer teaching possible. Publications and an interest in research necessary. South East Panhandle State University, in Grassland, Texas, (an equal opportunity employer) is a ranch-style university located high on the Caprock.

Except, knowing Tim, I figured he would find a way to include a line about a horse, a campfire, and a sunset into the ad: *South East Panhandle State University . . . a ranch-style university located high on the Caprock, where the campfires*

18

glow as the mustangs parade before fiery sunsets.

"Don't' worry, I don't need no stinking recommendation."

Tim was enough of a film buff to smile at the allusion to the famous line. He waved me out of the office past Doris and into the sunny north wind that seemed to never stop roaring in the Panhandle during the early spring.

Chapter 2
Learning Texas Pride

I met all of Jake's employees at his funeral. It was an odd affair conducted in the center drive of the Texas Pride Car Wash, the area between the wet bays where customers, even during the service, dropped coins into the safes and activated the timers that allowed them to high pressure their vehicles, and the dry bays, the covered vac area. It was a warm spring day; a storm had blown through overnight and the air was clear and clean and the traffic was unusually light on Cleburne Road. There was no casket, just a vase with Jake's remains which rested comfortably on the brick base of a vacuum cleaner. Jake had taken care of all the details for his service just like he had taken care of all the details involved with running Texas Pride. I had found the instructions for his funeral neatly filed with the other vital information in the *Maintaining Texas Pride* book. He kept the book in his "office," the room where he counted money, organized deposits, and paid bills and taxes.

Instead of a minister, Jake's across-the-street neighbor, Gene, a long-bearded forty year old, conducted the service, brief as it was. There weren't many of us in attendance. In addition to me and Gene, there was Linda and Doyle, the cleanup crew; Gary, the contract mechanic; Lloyd, the part-time location manager; and Gonzalo, who helped

Linda deal with the vacuums. The customers looked on at the service with curious eyes, letting the spray wands die in their hands as they listened to Gene, who I thought looked like Gandolf in a white Druid robe.

"We've gathered here, at Jake's special place, to say goodbye to our old friend, our friend Jake who spent many years on this lot maintaining his beloved Texas Pride Car Wash."

A cop car screamed down Cleburne Road, and Gene had to wait a moment to continue.

"Jake was never much on religion, so he simply asked that I hand over his remains to his nephew, Leonard, and give these bonus envelopes to his employees who were also his friends."

"Okay." Gary whispered.

There was a muted round of applause from the workers, none of whom were exactly dressed for the service. Gary, wearing his grease-stained clothes and a gimme cap embroidered with his philosophy of life, "Here for a Good Time, Not a Long Time," was the shabbiest of all. He was a stocky red-head with a full red beard. In his late fifties, Gary fit in well with his over-the-hill motorcycle buddies.

Linda wore clean rags, and her husband, Doyle, who seemed like a giant standing next to his petit wife, wore a fresh white t-shirt and pressed faded jeans. The clean up work never seemed to leave him dusty as he left most of the job to Linda. Lloyd, the part-time location manager whose main task was to stock the vending machines and test all the equipment, wore slacks and a dress shirt left over from his years with the Corps of Engineers. Gonzalo wore faded jeans and an extra large "I Survived the Summer of 2011" t-shirt that barely covered his beer gut.

But it was Gene, the shaman neighbor, who really

stood out in his white Druid outfit.

"Jake asked me to thank you all for your help during the past years. He left these for you."

Gene waved a handful of plain white envelopes.

"These are for Linda and Doyle, and this one's for Lloyd, and this one's for Gary, and this last one's for Gonzalo."

Gary took his envelope and ripped it open. Hundred dollar bills floated to the ground, and Gary rushed to gather them before some customer saw what had happened. Gonzalo stared at the bills like he had never seen folding money before. Linda and Lloyd respectfully folded the envelopes into their pockets and gave Gene their attention.

Gene handed me the vase with Jake's ashes. None of this made much sense to me, but I figured that the service must have been what Jake wanted since he had trusted Gene to distribute the bonus envelopes.

"All Jake said about the disposal of his remains was to be sure not to dump him in the pits," Gene said, nodding at the wet bays.

Much later I would have the remains interned next to Aunt Sue at Laurel Land Memorial Park.

"Although a skeptic, Jake came, in his last years, to believe more and more in mystery and less and less in mechanics," Gene continued, "and he asked that I finish the service with a special offering."

Gene walked to the wet bays with all of us close behind. When Jake had built the car wash, it had been an eight bay location, but since he walled in bay eight for a storeroom, there were only seven wet bays left. Gene went from bay to bay, dropping a silver quarter (one made before 1965) down each of the grated pits that collected run off water from the wash bays.

"With these seven silver quarters," Gene said, "I do hereby banish evil and angry spirits from this place, Jake's Texas Pride Car Wash at the corner of Cleburne Road and Berry Street in Fort Worth, Texas. Forevermore, the spirits that reside in this place will be kind ones."

Linda, Doyle, Gary, Gonzalo, and Lloyd headed for their vehicles.

"Hey, Leo," Gary said, "Don't forget that Friday is payday."

"And you'll need to rob the safes before the weekend," Lloyd said. "They're likely to fill up soon."

Gene shook my hand.

"Welcome to Texas Pride."

That evening, at Jake's house in Westcliff, I made dinner and drank one of Jake's beers. From what I found in the kitchen, beer and coffee were Jake's two most important foods. Jake was a simple soul who lived simply, and I worried that Gene, the shaman across the street, had taken advantage of my uncle in his advancing years. Jake and Sue had never been particularly religious, but I was pretty sure that Sue, had she been alive, would never allow a Druid to cross her door. And I knew that Sue would not have agreed to a pagan service for Jake. Later, I learned that Gene followed a career as a more traditional healer: a home healthcare nurse. Gene had apparently expanded his notion of health care to include magic and herbal remedies, especially the "medical" marijuana that he grew under lights.

Jake's place was perfectly designed for running a coin-op car wash. The alarm system never slept, surveillance cameras surveyed the front and back yards, bars protected the doors and windows, and there was a loaded gun in every room. I collected and unloaded all the weapons that I located

24

on my initial search—a couple of .38 revolvers, a .32 auto, and a short barreled 12 gage shotgun—and carefully laid them on the kitchen table. Jake had filled an entire bedroom closet with freeze dried food and ammo. Later, when I found the key to Jake's gun cabinet, I discovered two 9mm Glocks, more shotguns, and a .223 semi auto rifle.

My biggest find came when I was emptying a bedroom closet and separating Good Will clothes from trash. Disposing of my uncle's clothing and personal stuff was a very sad chore. It reminded me of having to deal with my folks' things when they died. I had made my way to the back of Jake's closet, finding some boots that might be Good Will worthy, when I accidentally leaned against the back wall of the closet while reaching for another pair of shoes. The wall shifted slightly when I touched it. I dumped the rest of the clothes from the closet and flashed a light on the wall. It was a painted sheet of plywood fitted tightly against the two-by-fours. I pried the plywood off the wall and shone my light on neat stacks of currency, wrapped in plastic and stuffed between the studs. I had discovered Jake's stash of cash: two hundred and fifty thousand in five dollar bills. Apparently, Jake believed in firepower and cash as well as magic. He was like one of the preppers in the end-of-the-world novels that I read.

When I first learned that Jake had dropped dead of a heart attack while sweeping up the lot at Texas Pride, I figured I could use my inheritance to escape the coming axe of being denied tenure at SEPSU. I never dreamed I would move into Jake's house, the house that Jake and Sue had lived in for so many years. But after finding the place clean, well organized, and secure, I decided to stay. The house was on the fringe of the Westcliff neighborhood, but on the poorer side, near Granbury Road and Seminary Drive.

After having spent years reading books and grading

papers, I found something refreshing in the concrete reality of the Texas Pride Car Wash. I knew the exterior layout well enough. There were eight covered dry bays, each with its own stainless steel vacuum cleaner. Every vac was mounted on a brick pedestal, and, since stainless steel had value, the vacs were welded to the I-beams that supported the roof. That kept the thieves from dragging vacs away behind a pickup truck. The eight dry bays faced seven wet bays equipped with high pressure soap and rinse, foamy brush, and low pressure tire/engine clean, presoak, and no-spot rinse. Jake had walled off the eighth wet bay that neighbored the animal hospital. He used that bay to store soap and supplies. Near to the storeroom was a vending island that sold car cleaning and air freshening products, as well as condoms. I soon discovered that condoms were one of Texas Pride's best selling vends. And on the far north side of Texas Pride the Dumpster anchored the lot with its dull, grey face that was colorfully scarred from the graffiti that never seemed to disappear, no matter how many times it had been erased.

While I had a fair understanding of the outside operations, the equipment room was a mystery to me: a labyrinth of tanks, hoses, wires, pumps, and motors. On each end of the equipment room was a bill changer, and both changers would accept ones and fives. Later, after reviewing the notes Jake had left me in his *Maintaining Texas Pride* book, I realized I could set a changer to take tens, twenties, and fifties, but that would set me up for theft via armed robbery (always a risk in a cash business) or by counterfeit or "strung" bills designed to trick the changers into dumping their coins.

Gary, who had his initial training with National Pride, the big chain of ten and twelve bays that had popped up everywhere in the 1970s, tried to explain the system to me, leading me through the equipment room so that I would have a basic understanding of what he called "the art and science of cleaning cars."

"Now this here is your water softener."

Gary lifted the black lid off a hundred gallon tank. The tank was half filled with salt nuggets.

"If you keep the water soft, you can mostly clean a car, even without soap or hot water. The soft water helps break the ionic charge that binds the dirt to the car surface. But if the water goes hard, cars won't come clean, and hard water clogs up the RO filter on the no-spot, and each filter costs $500, so we keep plenty of salt in the softener so it can cycle every other day. We also test the water hardness every day. We want to get a result of zero drops of hardness."

I nodded, pretending to understand what he was talking about, afraid to show my ignorance by asking what a RO filter was or what a water softness test kit looked like. I made a mental note to look up the mechanics in the *Maintaining Texas Pride* booklet.

"Of course, this is the hot water boiler, and your hot water holding tank off to the side here. And the air compressor," Gary said, pointing to a towering grey tank topped with a motor and belt pump, "powers the low pressure functions like tire clean, no-spot rinse, and foamy brush. See how the air hoses hook up to the holding tanks and bladders over there."

"Of course."

"And these here," Gary said, pointing to a row of seven pumps belted to seven motors bolted to seven steel pump stands, each with its own hydra of electric lines, "is what gives you the high pressure for the soap and rinse and wax functions. The five horse power motor—these are good ones, made in Brazil—spins the belt attached to the pump, and each

27

pump and motor runs a bay, so even if a couple break down you'll always have some bays open."

A motor and pump suddenly screamed to life with a shriek that made me jump.

"Oh, yeah. I usually wear hearing protection in here. And you want to watch them belts. Easy way to lose a finger, maybe even a hand, if you get caught in there when one of them is turning. Need to kill the power before messing with any motors or pumps or belts."

Gary pushed back his gimme cap ("Here for a Good Time, Not a Long Time") and threw me a sideways look.

"Maybe you should let me deal with all the high voltage issues until you get a better feel for the place."

"No problem."

"Eventually you'll need to learn some simple repairs. Changing pump belts, rebuilding a pump, replacing a burnt out vac motor. But Lloyd tests each machine every day, and he'll leave me a note if something needs fixing. You can learn a bit at a time by watching me."

We stepped out onto the lot. The traffic noise on Cleburne Road and Berry seemed slight compared to the roar of the equipment room. Gary proceeded to detail the operation of a wet bay: the customer dropped some coins (authenticity checked by a sensor and slugs rejected) into the timer (three minutes for a dollar), then selected the desired function on the rotary dial—wash, foamy brush, rinse, tire clean, presoak, no spot rinse.

People sometimes referred to self serve car washes as if they were dairy farms; the harvest was quarters, ones, and fives—a cash cow. Just then Lloyd drove up in his battered Chevy pickup.

"Don't let this drunk cowboy scare you."

Lloyd climbed out of his truck and winked at Gary.

"Hey, Lloyd. Finally decide to come to work? You know I can't repair nothing until you get here and mark it broke."

"I checked the lot early this morning," Lloyd said. "I just came by to explain the process of collecting to Leo."

"Yeah, well I was just explaining how the coins dropped through the timers into the safes."

Gary glanced at his watch.

"I'll let Lloyd tell you the rest. I've got three more locations to check. And the water heater's not working at Squirt, Wipe and Go."

Gary contracted at four locations, each of them run by a different owner. Squirt, Wipe and Go was Texas Pride's nearest competitor. It was an eight bay about four miles south on McCart, just before the street crossed I-20. I hadn't met the owner, but Gary said his name was Owen and that he was a gay guy who taught business at Tarrant County College. My old department head at SEPSU, Tim, would have called TCC a graveyard where adjuncts went to eat wood. Gary, who apparently had never heard of political correctness, just called it "Taco-Jacko U" because it was the college of choice for lots of poor Mexican-American kids and mediocre high school athletes who hadn't scored too well on the SAT. I found it interesting that another academic owned a coin-op car wash. Of course, Owen was a business professor, so it made a sort of sense that he would own a business. Still, I wondered about the name of his place, Squirt, Wipe and Go. But English professors often read too much into titles.

Gary drove off in his old red Toyota truck, and Lloyd took over as tour guide.

"Anyway," Lloyd continued, "you'll need to empty the bay safes at least once a week, and they're overdue now. The vacs really need robbing too. I've been collecting the coins from the vending machines. Got a pretty good bucket. Put it under the east changer. I'll be needing the red quarters from the safes as soon as you can separate them out. And the changers been empty for days now. You're sure to have a lot of bills."

"Red quarters?

"Yeah, Jake painted my test quarters so he could be sure I was testing the equipment every day. I suppose you want to do the same."

"Sure."

"Now keep on yellow when you rob them safes," Lloyd said. "Owen, the fellow that owns Squirt, Wipe and Go, he was held up a few months ago. But the creeps will probably still be looking for Jake, at least for a while."

I spent the evening reviewing the notes about collecting money that Jake had left in his book, *Maintaining Texas Pride*. He had obviously been making notes and writing articles and instructions in the large, loose leaf binder for a good number of years. Except for the chapter on "Weather and Texas Pride," none of the entries had dates, but every now and then Jake had pasted a newspaper article, usually one about the weather and car washing ("Ice Storm Leads to Busy Days at the Self-Serve") that indicated dates going back to 1978. *Maintaining Texas Pride* was a little more than a hundred pages (none numbered) long: page after page of lined double-spaced filled with Jake's neat cursive, the kind of writing they don't even teach anymore. (I recalled a thesis that argued that "Cursive Can't Be Creative" because it's formulaic.) I skimmed a few pages of *Maintaining Texas Pride*, and I found myself impressed with Jake's clean, no nonsense style. Even the punctuation, if he limited himself to simple and compound sentences, wasn't so bad.

Jake had made an extensive list of scheduled maintenance. There were daily chores (test all equipment with coins), weekly chores (empty vacuum debris bins and clean dust filters), and monthly chores (lubricate locks with graphite). The booklet also contained lists for annual and perform-as-needed maintenance. At least I would know what I was supposed to be doing in order to properly maintain Texas Pride.

There were actually quite a few pages concerning money, but I needed to learn how to fill the changers and open those safes, and I needed to learn fast, so I turned to the section of the manual titled "Collecting." In simple process-explanation style (one of my favorite types of essays to teach) Jake explained what I wanted to learn step-by-step:

"You'll find the combinations to the bay safes, the safe dial, and the keys to vac safes and the bill changers on the shelf in the gun cabinet," Jake had written. "Just take some buckets, the safe dial and combinations, a towel and some WD-40, and you're set to go. Remember, dial left-right-left, stop on the last number of the combination and press in the dial. The safe door will release but be careful, it's heavy and coins will spill out of the safe. Place the safe door on the ground, spray some WD-40 on the fittings, then scoop the coins into the bucket. You can use those coins to fill changers. Make certain you lock the safe by spinning that dial when you replace the door. And, yeah, watch your ass when your out on the lot with all that cash."

Early the next morning, following Jake's directions carefully, I loaded ten five-gallon aluminum buckets into the cab of his old pick up along with the safe dial and combinations. I drove to the lot, parked in bay four, and stared at the circled face of the stainless steel bay safe. It seemed to stare back a me, a dare: "Bet you can't get me open,

31

Buddy!"

I unlocked the equipment room and turned off the alarm that ran to the safes. The safe waited patiently for me in bay four as I fumbled with the dial and spun in the combination Jake had recorded. The safe face stared back at me, unmoved. I tried again and again and again to open it, carefully spinning the dial as Jake had instructed. A couple of early bird gangsters wrapping up a long night of "the life" pulled into the bay next to me and offered encouragement.

"Hey, man. You need some help with that?"

The dudes fired up a 7 a.m. joint and sat back in their car to enjoy the show. On attempt number ten, I somehow opened the safe and quarters spilled onto the lot, more than a few of them dropping into the grated drain in the center of the bay. The gangsters coughed and laughed, then finished their joint and sped away on Cleburne Road.

After an hour, I had robbed the four bay safes and collected from the eight vacs. Collecting from the vacs was much easier than collecting from the bay safes. To empty the coin boxes on the vacs required only a key and hands as strong as a "jaws of life" that the firefighters use. No one had collected at the location in the two weeks since Jake had died, and there were a lot of quarters, heavy quarters I soon discovered, in the buckets I had loaded into the cab of the pickup. I opened the changers, took the bills–there were several pounds of them–from the stackers, and filled the coin hoppers with quarters from the bay safes. I would worry about a count for the exchange another time. I set the alarm, locked the equipment room, and hurried to the truck. I drove off, doubled around the block on Gordon Avenue to be sure I wasn't being followed, and snaked my way home to count the loot.

Chapter 3
Money

Having money was a new experience. After all, I was just an English teacher living on a salary barely large enough to cover essentials plus beer and cable. Money for me arrived as an automatic deposit in my checking account once a month, a deposit that quickly evaporated when I paid rent, the car payment, and the minium on my credit card. Sure, I had a 403k, but the balance indicated that I would be eating either cats or cat food in my golden years. Then, suddenly, there was money, money, money, everywhere—not checks or auto deposits—but real money: coins and currency. Of course, Jake had anticipated the money issues and left special instructions in *Maintaining Texas Pride*.

"At first, you will think that dealing with the money is fun, but you'll soon discover that it is just work, the physical movement of an object or objects from one place to another. In our case, the objects are coins and bills which we will move from the Texas Pride location to the counting room where we will sort and count the currency and coins, write up the deposit slips, and finally carry the deposits to the bank."

There were instructions concerning how to separate the quarters into special canvas banking bags that held a thousand dollars each. Each thousand-dollar bag, I soon found out, weighed about fifty-four pounds.

Most evenings would find me in the workroom, really

just a spare bedroom with a counting table that held the coin and currency counters. I would wear earphones to cut the sound of the quarters hitting the counting bucket, pop open an IPA, and start shoveling quarters into the counter. The counter was a simple, spinning plate that lined up the coins and pushed them though a slot and into the bucket below. Each time a coin was pushed through the slot, the number on the counting dial would register the coin. Four thousand quarters made up a thousand dollar bank bag, and it took an hour and at least a couple of IPAs to count three or four of the thousand-dollar sacks. Jake was right, of course; except for the IPAs, there wasn't much fun in counting money.

And the quarters were just a part of the money counting situation. There were two bill changers at the Texas Pride location, and they had to be stocked with coins, and the bills, all ones and fives, had to be sorted and counted. I would very carefully separate the ones from the fives and stack them neatly. Then I would "spank" a couple of inches of bills by slapping the stacks against the desktop. Jake had described the process in his booklet. For some reason that he didn't explain, "spanking" the bills allowed them to be more easily fed into the currency counting machine. Every few days the money had to be deposited in the bank. I had left Jake's stash of cash hidden in the false closet wall, so I started holding back some of the five dollar bills that I collected from the changers. I wanted to build my own stash. Before long, I had forgotten how to use my ATM card and my credit card balance slowly began to dissolve.

I discovered that Gene felt it his neighborly duty to check in on me from time to time, which didn't brother me since I did so little socializing in my new car wash career. Because Texas Pride was open twenty-four hours a day, seven days a week, 365 days a year, I spent a lot of time taking care of the place. I ran into the crew—Linda and Lloyd and Gary and Gonzalo—every now and then, but beyond them my only pals were the clerks at the liquor stores where I bought my IPAs. Naturally, weekends and holidays, when "normal" folks had time off, were the busiest times at Texas Pride. Back at SEPSU, I was required to attend a reading or retreat or dinner every couple of weeks. But as manager and owner of Texas Pride Car Wash, I wasn't receiving many invitations to such events, and I hadn't gotten desperate enough to start attending the poetry readings that the TCU English department sponsored. So, I actually looked forward to spotting Gene heading my way, crossing the street with a drink in his hand.

"Anything I can do to help you over here?" Gene would ask.

"No, we're okay."

"Been a tough one for me," Gene said, taking a sip of his drink. "Got axed from another nursing gig. Super caught me smoking the good stuff during my break."

The "good stuff" was some of Gene's homegrown. I had seen the grow in a light-flooded room at the back of his house. ("Just for medicinal purposes," Gene explained.)

"Going to look for another job?"

"Probably not. I've still got several private clients to service. And I've decided to set up an ayahuasca retreat down in Big Bend. I'm going to sell this house and my collection of healing bowls and buy some property in Terlingua Ranch.

In addition to the grow room full of "medical" pot, Gene had a room full of Tibetan brass bowls and gongs, some of them actual antiques, that he used in healing ceremonies. Each bowl, when correctly rubbed, emitted a tone, and, according to Gene, each tone issued a vibration that had an unique healing property.

"Living is easy down in Big Bend. No one to bother you as you drink your ayahuasca and chase your spirit animal across the star drenched sky."

"You make it sound like a cowboy poem," I said.

"Oh it's poetic alright. But I've got to unload a troublesome bowl before I do anything else. I paid a fortune for it, but this bowl places a curse on its owner. It always brings bad luck. A competitor sold it to me even though he knew it was cursed, but I can't risk my karma by selling it to anyone who doesn't know its history."

"Bad, huh?"

"Really bad."

"Irritable bowl syndrome?"

"It's not a joke," Gene said. "I'll probably just dump it in a lake."

He had a long, bearded face and an open expression that made every question and statement sound sincere.

"I didn't mean to offend."

"You know, I did my apprenticeship with an native shaman down in Peru a few years back. I've been practicing for a couple of years, and I'm ready to expand. I'm going to call the place Desert Vision Retreat. Going to have a pool, above ground of course, and sweat lodge and all. You'll have to come down for a session."

"Don't see how I"ll ever get away from the job. Texas Pride never closes."

"Yeah. Jake was always talking about that, too."

"How did you come to know Jake so well, anyway?"

Gene pulled at his beard a moment.

"We were neighbors, of course. And I'd see Jake pull into the drive and haul buckets of coin into the house, and I'd say 'hello.' He was always a good neighbor, let me borrow the truck to buy some gardening supplies once. Some days we would just sit outside and talk over beers."

"I see."

"Yeah, we were both a bit lonely. I didn't know your aunt Sue. She had died before my wife bought the house."

"So you were married?"

"Yeah. She was a nurse too. She left me for a doctor, and Jake and I were the bachelors on the block."

That explained a lot.

"You been married?"

"No, but my last girlfriend, the one that got away, had been married once. She said marriage was not a safe haven but a voyage on uncharted seas, or something like that."

"Well, my marriage was more like a voyage on the Titanic. When you get hitched, I hope you have better luck than I had. Anyway, the last couple of years, I've been helping people with their ayahuasca experiences. Help them find their spirit animals, find themselves, cure whatever it is that's troubling them. I help folks expel the spirits that make them depressed or alcoholic or addicted. Sure, you might get a little sick. But throwing up is part of the journey. Expelling all the bad spirits is essential."

I had watched a Travel Channel show on a Canadian fellow who took ayahuasca in Peru. There was a lot of vomiting before the fellow wandered off into the jungle with his shaman guide.

"I'll think about it."

"I'll be around a while. Don't hesitate to ask if you need any advice, medical or otherwise. Matter of fact, it's been sort of lonely on the block since Jake passed."

Apparently, after Sue died, Jake had also been lonely, and that must have been the reason he befriended an outlier like Gene. I could understand how that could happen; car washing was, by nature, a lonely job, and most of the social interaction was of the negative sort. And Gene, crazy as he was, was harmless and entertaining.

Then Gene would disappear for a week or two before repeating the visits. As far as I could tell, he made his living selling pot and pills, but he did so discretely; there wasn't a lot of traffic or visitors at his house, so he was obviously providing delivery to his "private clients." I have to confess to buying some of his "good stuff" to help me through the chores of counting money and making deposits.

After I filled three or four canvas bags of quarters ($1000) per bag, I would truck them and a briefcase full of bundled fives and ones to the bank for deposit. Because the car wash generated such a large amount of cash, the bank allowed me to use the armored guard entrance. I would dolly my two-hundred-pound load of quarters from the truck to the door of the windowless building that housed the commercial section, and then I would ring the doorbell and wait for the tellers to check me out and buzz me into the outer area of the deposit room. Of course, the tellers were on the other side of bullet proof glass. More often than not, I would have to wait as the Brinks guys dropped off their loads. It was always fun to sit back on the worn leather couch and wait my turn as the guards hand wheeled a wagon filled with a million dollars in and out of the bank.

One afternoon when I had to make a currency deposit, I parked in the lot and walked around one the armored trucks just as the guards were rolling out a crate of cash. One of the guards drew his pistol as I raised my briefcase and my other hand to show my intentions were good.

"Please don't shoot me," I said. "I'm just trying to make a deposit."

The guard didn't lower his pistol. I recognized the other guard because I had seen him at the bank a few times.

"Come on, man. You've seen me here before."

Hands in the air, I stepped back to get out of their way as the guards lowered the tailgate of the truck and pushed the currency cart inside. The guard I knew stayed in the back with the bills, while the other guard, the driver, pistol now lowered to the 'ready" position, made his way to the cab of the armored car. After they drove off, I rang the bell and the tellers admitted me into the deposit room. I made a note to reschedule my deposits to avoid the armored car guys as well as the potential robbers.

Counting those thousand dollar bags of quarters and sorting and counting all the ones and fives (even with the help of the coin and currency counting machines) was boring but exacting because the bank charged a fee if a deposit were off. Every now and then something "exciting" would happen: a bent coin or a slug would jam the coin counter or a five strung with dental floss would show up in the currency. The dental floss was evidence that someone was trying to "string" the change machine by inserting a bill into the validator, which triggered the coin release, and then retrieving the bill by pulling it out of the validator with the string. This was an old trick that might have worked back in 1985, but all the twenty-first century changers had safeguards that prevented this fraud.

One evening after I had finished counting the quarters and had started sorting the massive pile of ones and fives, I noticed that some of the bills had writing on them. I began a collection of these inscribed bills. There were a lot more of them than I had first noticed. Most often, the message (always in cursive, sometimes in red ink) was superstitious: "write this on ten more bills and you will be rich," or "the next person to receive this bill will be famous," or simply "good luck from Gzim." Sometimes the messages were love notes:

"Erica loves someone special," or "*Te amo, te adoro.*" Sometimes the message was a prayer: "Give my partner health in Jesus name, give back in body what Satan has took," or "in Jesus name I can do all things." Sometimes the message was a warning: "Danger—Grapevine police molest teen female drivers. Warn others!"

As a former English professor, I found this faith in the communicative power of currency intriguing. I could smell an academic paper or even a monograph on the subject: "The Hidden Literature of Money: Superstition, Love, Prayer and Protest." It seemed crazy at first, but I had noticed the messages on the bills even when the bills were only a few among thousands that I counted every month. Would the "ordinary" person using transaction cash read the scribbling on the currency? I considered using one dollar bills—I always had a few thousand of them lying around—as composition paper. Maybe the value of the paper bill would make my writing more valuable? I imagined a novel written on pasted together ones, sort of like the rolled manuscript that Jack Kerouac used in *On the Road*.

I took a fresh one from a stack of bills on the table, and, using a bold red marker wrote "Just say 'no' to cowboy poetry" across the face of George Washington. I took a fresh looking five and wrote "*Te amo*, Pam!" across Lincoln's frosty gaze. I immediately felt better, more powerful, a criminal for defacing currency while self publishing my literary criticism and declaring my love for Pam. I replaced the bills into the stack and bound them for deposit, wondering if these notes tossed into the green sea of the Federal Reserve would find readers.

Of course, with money came problems. Not just the problems of collecting and counting, but also the problems of making sure no one else got the money. The "bad guys" made

nearly constant attempts to gleam some cash from Texas
Pride. If they couldn't get the cash, they often went for
something else. In fact, everything that could be stolen off the
lot had been stolen at one time or another. Jake had noted in
Maintaining Texas Pride that he had been forced to chain all
the grates covering the drain pits to the foundation of the
building. That was because one night the scrap metal bandits
took all of the grates off the bays and by dawn three cars had
fallen into the pits. According to Jake's notes, no one was hurt
but there was a lot of damage and a couple of law suits as
result of the theft. But there were other, more serious
criminals to worry about. The car wash was something like a
bank; it was where the money was, and that attracted a lot
attention.

Unlike Owen, my competitor at Squirt, Wipe and Go, I
had yet to experience the thrill of an actual armed robbery,
but I expected one every time I stepped onto the lot. With all
that money around, I tried to be on *red* most of the time. I
made a habit of circling the place before getting out of my truck.
If I spotted anyone hanging out in the alley between the vet's
animal hospital and the convenience store or if there were too
many gangsters on the lot, I just drove on and returned later.
I began collecting money in the mornings, but never at exactly
the same time, on the theory that most of the trouble makers
would be sleeping off their hangovers. It was the danger of
armed robbery that led me to take a greater interest in Jake's
gun collection.

When I taught at SEPSU, I didn't own a gun.
However, there was gun play in a classroom the year before I
resigned. It happened in my colleague's Intro to Rhetoric
class, ironically enough just after an energetic discussion of
various gun control issues. It was Texas, so guns were always
a topic of discussion, including whether or not students with

41

permits should be allowed to carry in their college classes. Professor Yata had taught at SEPSU for decades and was approaching retirement. For him, the Caprock region was attractive because it was close to Colorado, and, back when he began his career at SEPSU, you could only get Coors beer in a few counties in Texas. Yata had a taste for Coors, and I'd seen him down a six pack at more than one party. His huge consumption of Coors was probably the reason he weighed 350 pounds and looked sort of like a grey-headed bowling ball. Professor Yata had just concluded the discussion, which he later claimed concerned the "shooting yourself in the foot" fallacy, when Mary, a sophomore from Dalhart, dropped her purse and BANG—a .25 caliber bullet whizzed past Yata's ear and into the blackboard behind him.

Since there were no injuries and it was clearly an accident and since it was west Texas, Yata confiscated the pistol, waved Mary away, and dismissed class, figuring he had better write up some sort of report on the incident. He stopped by the English department office to check his mail and went home for the weekend. That was the last time I saw Professor Yata, and I only learned about the shooting the following week. The headline of the two-page weekly campus paper, *The Caprock Rock Hound*, summed up the narrative as only college journalists can: "Argument about gun control leads to shooting in English class." Five paragraphs into the story, I learned that the shooting was accidental and no one was hurt, but that Professor Yata had taken "emotional recovery" leave in Golden, Colorado, and was planning to retire at the end of the semester.

So guns, for me, were exotic, hazardous objects better left alone. But then I inherited Texas Pride and Uncle Jake's gun collection. For Jake, guns were simply tools; he had a gun for each task or chore. For home defense, there was the .12

gage pump. For concealed carry, I had the choice of a Smith and Wesson "Chief's Special," which was a five-shot stainless steel revolver chambered in .38 special, a 9mm Glock 26, what some folks called the "baby" Glock, or the Beretta .32 semi-auto pocket rocket. There was also a .357 Smith and Wesson revolver and a Glock 17 in 9mm, good guns to have in the house or car. For any thing else, there was the AR 15 in .223 caliber. I unloaded and locked away all of these except for the "Chief's Special" revolver; it came with a inside-the-belt holster, and it was compact and simple to use—just pull, point, and shoot. Even an English teacher could figure it out.

To be on the safe side, I took a few lessons at the local firing range before I started carrying on the Texas Pride lot. The range, Shooter's Palace, was conveniently located in a revamped warehouse just south of downtown, only a few miles from the Texas Pride location. My instructor was Clint, a fifty-five year-old retired cop who, in addition to providing training sessions at Shooter's Palace, sometimes worked private security for the Bass family, the richest family in Fort Worth. Clint had close cut brown hair, clear brown eyes, and apparently, judging by his physique, spent a lot of time working out in the gym. If he had been a foot taller he could have been a stand in for that other, more famous Clint, that Eastwood fellow.

"So, you know anything about guns or pistols?"

"Not really. I fired a .22 rifle once in Boy Scouts."

"That's good," Clint said, nodding his head. "I won't have to make you unlearn all the bad habits you picked up on your own. What type gun are you planning to shoot?"

I handed him the .38 Chief's Special in its holster. Clint unholstered the pistol, clicked the cylinder open, and examined the gun to be sure it was unloaded.

"The stainless steel model. Good choice. Simple to use

and clean, extremely reliable, and easy to conceal carry. Just remember, safety first. Forget the single action function," Clint said, pulling back the hammer. "Your trigger pull is a lot lighter in single action, but it's asking for an accident."

Clint used his thumb to slowly lower the hammer.

"This double-action revolver has no safety. You just point and pull the trigger and that's it. Double action, when you pull the trigger without cocking the hammer, is probably about twelve pounds. Pretend there is a laser light coming from the barrel of the pistol. Never let that beam cross anything you don't want to destroy. Always act if the pistol is loaded, even if it isn't, and don't put your finger on the trigger until you are ready to fire."

He handed the pistol back to me and took a box of ammo and a target from the shelf behind his gun display counter. It was a circle target, not one of the poster sized bad-guy targets.

"When we get into the range, I want you to load the pistol and assume this two handed stance."

He bent slightly at the knee, made a finger pistol with his right hand, and braced his right wrist with his left hand.

"Notice I've got my left foot a little further forward than the right foot, and I've got the pistol hand braced to keep my aim steady. Knees are slightly bent, relaxed. There's not much sight on your little baby, but when the blade on the front sight fills the notch in the rear just in front of the hammer, you are on target. Of course, you won't be making any long shots with this two inch barrel. Come on. We'll try her out."

We donned our hearing protection and entered the first door to the firing range. This door opened into a glass-walled, closet-sized room that created an air lock that protected the gun shop from noise and lead. Even with ear protection on, I could hear the BANG! BANG! BANG! of the shooters firing on the range. Another door opened up onto ten shooting alleys, all separated by three inches of bulletproof glass and each equipped with a push button target line that was automatically set to five, ten, fifteen, twenty, and twenty-five yards. That first day we only fired twenty rounds at the five-yard target. Even that made my hand ache. Over the next few weeks, with more practice, I felt at ease with the .38 and began to carry it in a waistband holster everywhere I went. Eventually, Clint trained me on the Glocks and most of Jake's other guns. I was becoming more and more like my uncle the longer I tried to maintain Texas Pride.

Fort Worth being Fort Worth, there were always a few armed robbers around town; it had been that way since the early days. Established as a fort in 1849, the town grew up rough. Named after General William Worth, a hero of the Battle of Chapultepec, Fort Worth boomed with the cattle industry and became the hangout for outlaws such as Butch Cassidy and his Hole in the Wall gang. Butch and his boys enjoyed the delights of "Hell's Half Acre," a famous strip of bars and brothels that wasn't closed until 1917 when Camp Bowie opened and the miliary shut down the red light zone in order to protect young recruits. And in the 1950s Jacksboro Highway (AKA Thunder Road) was lined with strip joints (Skyliner Ballroom featuring Candi Barr), gambling dens (The Four Duces), and dance halls (The Rocket Club).

Those days were long gone when Paul Theroux, whose books I sometimes taught in my Contemporary American Lit class, visited Fort Worth while traveling from Boston to South America in *The Old Patagonian Express: By Train Through the Americas*. Theroux debarks in Fort Worth and is shocked to see a convenience store door greeting him with a picture of a double barrel shotgun and a sign declaring that an "Armed Officer" might be on guard. That was back in the early 1970s, and things hadn't gotten any better since Paul's visit. Most of the contemporary robbers seemed to concentrate on sandwich shops and convenience stores. (How desperate did one have to be to rob a sandwich shop, anyhow?) In fact, Owen, my competitor at the Squirt, Wipe, and Go car wash had recently been relieved of several thousand in ones and fives by three guys in blue jeans, grey hoodies, and face masks; one of them flashed a Glock.

Most of the criminals, however, were not brazen armed robbers. They worked by stealth, taking advantage of any carelessness and constantly trying to trick the changers or to break into the vac or bay safes. A lot of the crime was seasonal. Jake wrote about it all in the *Maintaining Texas Pride* booklet. Of course the holidays were always bad, what with everyone short of money. And then it was Stock Show season. Fort Worth hosts the Stock Show every February (it used to be known as the Fat Stock Show back when fat was more prevalent on cows than people), and that's when the most talented thieves, the carneys who traveled the circuit, would try to cheat the bill changers out of all their quarters or pick the locks on the safes. The carneys have a natural cover; they move from town to town, making a score and then leaving before anyone can tie them to a crime.

The "smartest" theft I experienced happened at Easter. There had been just enough rain that week to get the cars dirty, and we had been busy before the holiday. When things got busy, I tried to rob the safes before someone else could get them. Just after dawn on Easter morning, even before Paul, the vet, was at his animal hospital waking his dogs, I pulled into bay one and parked by the safe. After a quick visit to the equipment room to turn off the alarm, I got my bucket and my safe dial, took a look around the lot, and spun the combinations into the lock with ease. All the weeks of practice with the safes was paying off, and I could now spring the disk doors easily.

I balanced my five gallon bucket against the wall, beneath the safe, which I expected to be almost full. But when I freed the safe door, the vault was nearly empty. Instead of a thousand dollars worth of quarters, there were only a few dozen coins. Someone had opened the safe and cleaned it out during the night, but the alarm had not sounded. This had never happened before to me, and later I confirmed that Jake never recorded such an incident in *Maintaining Texas Pride*. The other safes were also nearly empty.

It didn't take long for me to discover the problem. Using a locksmith's tool, the criminals had opened the door to the meter box which contained the low voltage wiring to the selection dial, a timer, and the chute where the coins dropped into the safe. I didn't alarm the meter box doors because customers were always banging on them if there were a problem or a coin jam. Only the safe doors were alarmed. Best as I could figure, the crooks had opened the meter boxes and snaked a vacuum down the coin drop into the safes.

Of course, there was no way to be sure, but I suspected that the crime was the work of Travelers from White Settlement; it was their sort of smart theft. The White Settlement Travelers were an group of Irish "walking people" who had made the Fort Worth suburb their home since the late nineteenth century. They were a closed society that shunned communication with outsiders and were rumored to practice arranged child marriage. They wintered in White Settlement mobile home parks and, during the warmer months, traveled the country looking for work, usually construction and roofing scams. The Travelers had a well established reputation for being con artists but had made the news in recent months for more serious crimes. These crooks were probably in a van using some type of generator to power the vac. I was impressed, and I guessed they scored about four or five thousand in coin.

The solution was simple: I could wire the meter box doors to the alarm system that would sound and call me if a meter box opened. But that would mean a lot of false alarms. I finally decided to weld a baffle in the safes just below the coin drop. That way, the baffle would block the vacuum hose and prevent the theft. The vacuuming thieves were pretty clever, unlike the majority of the criminals that assaulted the wash.

The more brazen criminals would go for the changers directly, usually late at night. Sometimes these attempts caused a lot of damage, especially if the crooks tried to pull the changer out of the wall with a chain attached to a truck. Nothing spoiled my third IPA and a dose of Gene's "medical" pot more than the alarm going off at the car wash. It always started with a recorded phone message: "Attention, emergency. The alarm is sounding at Texas Pride Car Wash. Send help immediately." The reason for the automated call was that Jake had set the system up so it would not call the police. That way, Jake couldn't be charged for all the "false" alarms. Most of the "false" calls, however, were real break in attempts, but the alarm would scare off the bad guys long before the cops, or I, arrived. At least that's what I kept telling myself.

The phone would ring—"Attention, emergency"—I would grab the .12 gage, tuck the .38 into my belt, and respond. I could be at the wash in seven minutes, enough time to allow the criminals an escape window. I usually parked across the tracks in the old post office lot and scanned the Texas Pride Wash with binoculars before heading over. So far, every time I had responded to an alarm the lot had been empty, just the grimy shadows in the all too dim security lights. I dreaded the day when I actually found someone on the lot breaking into something.

One night I hurried to Texas Pride in response to an alarm to find a police car on the lot and the front door of the equipment room that housed the changers bent off its hinges by a pickup truck, obviously stolen, that had been rammed into it. Repairs cost more than what money the bad guys would have gotten if they had been successful.

Lots of the things people stole were small, items that before I inherited the car wash I could never imagine anyone taking. One of the first things I did when I took over the lot was a beatification project. I hired Gonzalo, who often helped Linda and the clean up crew service the traps on the vacs, to plant a couple of flower beds on the border of the wash. Gary, the mechanic, laughed when he saw us working on the project.

"Leo, that's not the way to run a wash. Those beds will be tore up in no time. People will drive through them. They'll be shitting in them, pissing in them, puking in them, leaving needles in them—no telling what. Flowers at a self serve car wash. You been at the college, smoking that wacky weed too long, *amigo*."

But I think even Gary was surprised when we arrived the next morning to discover that all the flowers Gonzalo had planted had been dug up: stolen.

Sometimes the criminals were working for you. That was what happened in the case of the forty thousand dollar tamales. I don't really know how much those tamales cost. It could have been fifty thousand or even more, or it could have been considerably less, somewhere in the ten thousand dollar range. There was no way to calculate the loss exactly because I was uncertain of how long the thefts had been taking place. Apparently, they had been going on long before I inherited Texas Pride from Uncle Jake. One thing I did know: those were damn good tamales.

Gonzalo had worked for Jake several years, and Gonzalo liked beer, Keystone Light. I knew that because I had seen him buy twelve packs at the *Mas Ramblas* across Gordon Avenue or the *tienda* next to Texas Pride. I had less day-to-day contact with him than with any of the other employees. I saw Linda and Doyle, the clean up crew, a couple of times a week, early in the mornings, and I was likely to run into Gary, the mechanic, at least once during the week, usually when something I couldn't fix broke on a weekend. And Lloyd, who was retired from the Corps of Engineers, was always around looking for something to do. So all I knew about Gonzalo was that he drank Keystone Light, drove a bad-ass car, and always wore faded jeans and an extra large t-shirt with some striking phrase inked across the front. These were clever sayings, like *I Survived the Summer of 2011, It's Your Lucky Day: I Like Fat Chicks,* or, *It Seemed Like a Good Idea at the Time.* I could rely on Gonzalo do some light clean up every afternoon ($10 a day, verbal contract, cash payment weekly), and he was also responsible for cleaning out the vac traps; payment was all the coins and valuables he found each week.

Everybody loved Gonzalo because his wife made dozens of tamales for the holidays, especially Christmas and *semana santa*, and Gonzalo would generously distribute them to the Texas Pride Crew. Now that Jake was gone, his share of the tamales went to me.

In Texas, following the tradition in the old country, Mexicans would gather for a *tamalada*, an event where the tamales were made and consumed. The men would drink beer while the women would knead the *masa*, then stuff tamales and wrap them in corn husks for steaming. The women filled the tamales with pulled pork, chicken, vegetables or any combination of those ingredients. Some people thought that a tamale that included an olive in it forecast fertility. The ones Gonzalo gave me were chicken, no olives. I'm sure they were among the best tamales in the state, and I'm certain they were the most expensive.

I was standing outside of the equipment room at the Texas Pride when Gonzalo drove up in his jet back 1980 Impala. I remember that even then it seemed odd to me that Gonzalo could afford to restore the car to its original glory and beyond, but I figured he sold drugs or something on the side. The Impala was customized and low slung on special shocks, the rear always sagging and threatening to "spark" the pavement.

Gonzalo got out of the Impala with a foil-wrapped plate of tamales. He was wearing loose jeans and a *I♥Bacon* t-shirt.

"*Hola*, Leo," he said, handing me the still warm plate. "My wife made these for you."

"Thank her for me, please."

I locked the tamales in my truck and finished collecting from the vac safes, which seemed to have fewer quarters than I expected. I drove the coins and the tamales home. I stashed the tamales in the fridge, took the coins to the counting room, and picked up the weekly pay envelope for Gonzalo. I opened the unsealed envelope and double counted the fives: $70, ten dollars a day for light clean up on the lot. I added four more five dollar bills and sealed the envelope. I decided to drive the pay over to Gonzalo's home, announce his raise, and thank his wife for the wonderful tamales that had lifted my spirts.

I had been out to Gonzalo's place a couple of times before to deliver his pay (always cash, no social or medicare deductions). Gonzalo and his family lived just off Seminary and Hemphill, an area that had become mostly Mexican in the last few decades. I drove by Rosemont school and the athletic fields on the north side of the street. There were lots of kids playing soccer. The neighborhood around the school was mostly composed of small, single family frame houses, some with cars out front. The area had changed a lot over the years. Once there had been a lake, Katy Lake. When I-35 opened, the lake was drained and the location became Fort Worth's first shopping mall, Seminary South. Now the mall had been renamed *Mercado Fiesta*.

As I made my way to Gonzalo's house, it occurred to me that except for the fact that the streets were paved and that I could drink the tap water I might have been somewhere in central Mexico. Every billboard was in Spanish, every strip mall had a *tienda* and a *taqueria*, diapered children shared fenced-in back yards with the family chickens, and stray dogs staggered down the alleys like starving drunks.

A lot of the older people, and some younger ones, too, resented the "invasion," as they called it. Somewhat selfishly, I saw the influx of newcomers as a good thing. Most of the customers at Texas Pride were Hispanic. And, with the exception of a few gang members, they were friendly, frugal people who took good care of their cars and would rather use the Texas Pride equipment for $3.50 than drive through a tunnel wash for $15. Besides, I was a Naturalist, not a nationalist. I realized that borders were artificial constructs, futile attempts to control inevitable migrations.

Gonzalo's freshly paved street, like all the streets in the neighborhood, was lined with parked cars and trucks, so much so that I had to park half way down the block from Gonzalo's place. I got out of the pickup and was grateful to have the new sidewalk since the street was cluttered.

As I walked up to Gonzalo's house, I saw him in the drive way, hovering over the open trunk of his old Impala. He was bent down, almost drooping, struggling with something heavy. He never saw me coming up behind him as he grunted and lifted until he got a bucket of quarters out of the trunk and onto the drive. A few quarters bounced out of the bucket and rolled across the street.

"*Chingadera*," Gonzalo muttered as he turned to look for the quarters he had dropped. Then he saw me.

"*Hola, jefee*," he said. He tried to stand in front of the bucket of quarters.

"So how long have you been stealing from Texas Pride? Were you skimming quarters when Jake was around?"

"You're wrong. Jake gave me these," Gonzalo said.

"Yeah, sure. And you've been carrying them around in your trunk for weeks?"

Gonzalo said nothing; he just stood there sweating in his bacon-loving shirt.

"Well, I'll change the locks on the door and the vac safes, so you're finished."

He stood defiant, a giant of fat, legs protecting the bucket of quarters. The front door of the house swung open and a Mexican even bigger than Gonzalo stomped out onto the porch.

"*Esta bien, hermano?*"

"You don't want to fight with us," Gonzalo said. "Just leave us be."

I pushed him aside, amazed at how spongy his flesh

felt against my hand. He fell hard against the Impala. I took the bucket by its handle and started down the sidewalk. Gonzalo's brother lumbered down the stairs.

"Tell him to back off," I said. "I'm not calling the cops, not unless I see you again on the lot. And thank your wife for the tamales."

Gonzalo bounded to his feet, his brother now at his side. They must have been twins as they both wore the same frustrated expression on their faces.

I carried the heavy bucket, probably five hundred dollars worth of quarters, back to my truck, again grateful for the beautiful sidewalk the city had installed. I didn't call the cops, and I never saw Gonzalo again, but, from that time on, I often thought of the tamales when the holidays came around.

Chapter 4
Weather and Texas Pride

As the chunks of ice fell from the sky, I opened the passenger door to my pickup and waved the woman and child into the cab.

"Come on. *Pase.*"

I had seen the woman and the little girl waiting for the bus when I had pulled into the bay to check the location only fifteen minutes earlier. They climbed into the cab.

The ice beat down, denting the roof of the wash bay. One baseball-size hailstone bounced off the hood of my pickup, leaving a scar. Cars pulled into the lot, crowding into the shelter of the bays, and the hail begin to whiten the street. On Cleburne Road, a truck jumped the curb, its windshield shattered by ice. The woman and I didn't bother to talk; the pounding of the hail on the roof of the bay made talking impossible. The little girl covered her ears with her hands. The ice crashed down like shrapnel.

The only people who pay more attention to the weather than the owners of car washes are the on-air professionals. In fact, I had been watching the weather closely all afternoon as the sky darkened and the bright red bands inched from west to east across the radar screen. I had decided to make a last minute check on the location, but the storm moved in faster than I expected.

Jake had even included a special section on weather in *Maintaining Texas Pride*. Most of the weather entries had to do with some event that affected the car wash income: dust and mud storms that left every car in town splattered with a patina of dirt, and ice storms, which guaranteed at least two weeks of good business as customers tried to get the road salt off their cars. And there were always the droughts, the deep freezes, and the extended periods of heat.

The ice finally stopped falling and the temperature dropped. Green-tinged clouds raced from west to east in the wake of the storm.

"*Gracias,*" the woman said.

She smiled and helped her daughter down from the cab. They began walking, slowly, hand in hand because of the hail-covered sidewalk and street, north on Cleburne Road, past the bus stop and across the street toward *Mas Ramblas*, the drive through beer joint.

I did a quick walk around the lot, looking for damage. The sheet metal roofs over both the wet and dry bays were heavily dented by the hail, as was the warp-around facade on the wet-bay roof, but that damage was only cosmetic. The cars on the lot didn't fare so well. Most of them had at least one window or windshield shattered by the ice. So far as I could tell, no one was hurt.

Once the hail melted off the streets, business began to boom, not with people washing their cars, but with people vacuuming the broken windshield glass from the car interiors. Seeing the cars begin to line up at each of my vacs, I headed back to the home office for my collection buckets and the tools I'd need to clear the vac traps which were sure to fill up with broken windshield glass. Cleaning vac traps was a job I usually farmed out to Linda and her crew, but the boom in business demanded that I do the dirty work myself.

Driving through the neighborhood, I could see that the damage was widespread: cars and houses with broken windows, a roof blown half off of a convenience store, tree branches down on the streets. It was a miracle that the power was still on. If the power went out, I would have to stay on the lot waving potential customers away. I was always amused when people would get upset at me because the power was out, as if I would kill the power to my own business just to delay their pressing need to hose down some old junker.

When I got home, I checked for storm damage. The burglar bars had protected the windows, but the house would need a new roof. Probably every house in Tarrant County would need a new roof. I got my collection keys and buckets as well a some leather gloves and a small shovel and drove back to Texas Pride.

The wash bays were empty, but the lines of cars at the vacuums snaked off the lot and onto the adjacent streets. I spent the afternoon emptying out the vac trash bins (if they were full of glass, the vacs would fail to suck) and collecting the money from each of the eight vac safes. I was charging fifty cents for a three minute vac, and the safes could each hold about three hundred dollars in quarters. As usual, I carried my .32 auto in my pocket and my .38 in a waistband holster. In spite of heavy use, the vacs held up well; I only had to replace one burnt out motor and free the jams in a few hoses. I emptied the safes every couple of hours; it was going to be a record day for the vacs, which, next to the vending machines that dispensed air freshener, towels, and condoms, were the highest profit machines on the lot. As I loaded the buckets of quarters into my truck, it occurred to me that, if you're a car wash man, even hailstorms can have a silver lining.

The hailstorm made me think of some of the other weather events Jake had recorded in the *Maintaining Texas Pride* journal. Of course, Jake was a native Texan, and Texans had a sense of pride about everything associated with their state, including the weather. Texas was a land of epic hurricanes, tornadoes, and floods; a place where droughts lasted years, heat waves melted the highways, and deep freezes shattered plants, animals, people, and equipment. Yet even when Fort Worth was silenced by white cold, the grapefruit grew in the Valley and bikini-clad college girls walked the beach at South Padre.

As the new owner of Texas Pride Car Wash, I found that my exposure to weather was much greater than I had expected. Naturally, I had seen some weather when I had taught at South East Panhandle State in Grassland, but I spent most of those Panhandle winters reading post-apocalyptic fiction and "advising" my favorite grad student. In the summers, Pam and I headed for the Colorado Rockies where you didn't even need AC. Besides, all my classes were in a modern, red brick building that was overheated in the winter and frosty cold in the summer, so once I made my way to campus from my double wide on the edge of town, I was pretty much sheltered. But at Texas Pride, the weather could not be so easily avoided or ignored. Working the Texas Pride Car Wash simply strengthened by belief in Naturalism by illustrating that nature and weather are indifferent to people and machines.

Jake had noted in *Maintaining Texas Pride* that ice storms were the most serious of the weather threats, at least from a car washing point of view. Sure, there would be dirty cars lined up at the wash bays for two weeks after a good ice storm, but before you could wash cars you had to have power, and ice storms could easily knock the power out for days. And to keep the equipment from freezing if an ice storm did knock out the electricity, Jake had installed a gas space heater that would insure the temperature in the room would stay at least forty, protecting the pumps and storage vats from cracking.

After I stacked the buckets of quarters (six buckets at about $500 a bucket meant at least $3,000—a new one day vac record) in the counting room and popped open a beer, I glanced though Jake's chapter on weather.

The chapter on the weather was one of the longest ones in the *Texas Pride* booklet and the only one that was arranged in chronological order. The first entries described the New Year's Eve ice storm of December 31, 1978, a storm that shut down Dallas and Fort Worth for days. Jake wrote that he "couldn't drive the streets so I walked to check the location. Just about froze my ass. Power was out but the space heater was holding the equipment room to 47 degrees. Weep system to each of the wet bays was working, keeping the water lines from freezing." And then, several days later: "After the thaw business boomed. Had to rob the safes each day cause they were filling up."

Business wasn't so good during the legendary heat wave of the summer of 1980. Jake wrote that "it's been over a hundred with no rain for more than forty days, hit 112 twice, and the temperature in the equipment room topped 130. When I come by, twice a day, I make sure I leave a large ice chest filled with bottled water by the equipment room door. This way people can get water without fooling with the automatic shut off on the outside sink facet. Been doing this for two weeks and no one's stolen the ice chest yet. I'm surprised."

There was a *Star-Telegram* clipping from 1995 about the hail storm that had destroyed Mayfest that year, and another clipping about the heat wave of 2011.

In the months that I had owned the car wash, I had been surprised by the weather several times. Twice, I had been forced to take cover in the equipment room when the tornado sirens sounded, and once I had narrowly avoided being swept down Cleburne Road during a flash flood.

But even more surprising than the weather were the people. One hundred degree heat index? No problem! I'm waxing the sports car. Rain falling? Won't stop me from using the tire cleaner! Freezing with a twenty-mile north wind. I'm soaping the sucker down anyway! People love their cars. Lots of important life events happen in cars; sometimes the only relationship people had was with their cars. And the way things had been going, more than a few people had resorted to calling their cars home.

The last entry Jake had made about the weather concerned a storm that swept through right before he died. I vaguely remembered the storm that Jake wrote about. It was a mud-dust storm that hit Grassland, where the college is, just hours before blowing into Ft. Worth. This was a rare weather event that combined elements of a dust storm with a thunderstorm. The rains fell through the blowing dust, forming blobs of brown mud that splattered all the cars to Jake's great delight.

In the other room the television blared a bleak teaser: "Dozens injured in worst hail storm since Mayfest 1995, details at ten."

I picked up a pen and made an entry in the Texas Pride weather log, starting where Uncle Jake had left off and trying to echo his prose style: "May hailstorm blows out windshields, damages buildings. TV reports it was the worst hailstorm since the 1995 Mayfest event. Record one day vac take due to the broken windshield glass."

I had made my first contribution to *Maintaining Texas Pride.*

60

Chapter 5
Sex and the Self Serve Car Wash

On Sundays, when the weather was good, I liked to check out the location early in the morning before business really got going, and often as not, Paul, the vet next door, would be across the fence walking one of his charges. Paul was a big fellow, with thick brown hair and hands that seemed too large for a vet. He was my pal; like me, he had to work 365 days a year. The animals never took off. He and his wife were religious, but he checked the hospital and kennel early each Sunday morning before church. That Sunday, Paul was sipping coffee and watching a young, unleashed spaniel that was wearing the "cone of shame." I was policing the fence line for trash.

There hadn't always been a fence between our properties. According to the notes Jake left me in the *Maintaining Texas Pride* booklet, Paul had installed the fence (a chain-linked twelve footer with spikes, but no barbed wire) about ten years back after one of the car wash customers assaulted one of Paul's employees and stole a full breed boxer. Paul ran the fence all along his property line, separating his hospital from the car wash, the alley behind Carshon's Deli, and the drive through beer window that pretended to be a convenience store. Thanks to the fencing, Paul and his employees could let the dogs out to sun in the afternoon without worrying about the animals escaping or being taken by people at the car wash. I am certain that Paul's employees were happy to have something besides thin air between them and the Texas Pride lot and the alley. The fence had become a wire curtain between the vet's and the rougher world. Besides for the closet-sized *tienda* selling cigs and beers from a drive through on the alley side, and Carshon's Deli, a long-time Fort Worth hangout, there weren't many businesses left open on our block of Cleburne Road. Sometimes a few homeless folks and drug addicts camped out in the alley, and the manager at Carshon's would call the cops and have them rousted.

Carshon's was a Fort Worth institution. The deli was originally located downtown; then in the 1950s it moved to Berry Street to be near TCU. In the early 1970's, Carshon's opened the current location on Cleburne Road, just south of Berry. At that time, the Texas Pride lot was a dry cleaners. When the dry cleaners burnt down, Jake bought the lot and started to build the car wash, which he opened in late 1978. In 1978, Cleburne Road was a promising location in the shadow of TCU, which owned a lot of the buildings on neighboring Berry Street. Recently, there had been talk at the regional planning meetings about tearing down some buildings on Cleburne and Berry to make room for a light rail development that would run directly downtown from the south side. There was the real possibility that some day Texas Pride and Carshon's would be leveled to make way for a rail line or easement.

"You should be pretty busy today," Paul said.

"Hope so. Slight chance of rain late afternoon."

A red Mustang convertible pulled into the vac bay nearest us, and Paul nearly dropped his coffee as a twenty-something blonde in a low-cut red sun dress and cowboy boots got out of the car. She deposited fifty cents into the vac and began vacuuming the front seat, giving us both a good view of her thonged behind. She shifted to the other side of the car to vac out the passenger's seat, flashing her braless breasts as she worked the vac cuff back and forth across the leather car seat.

"She must really want a clean car to be out this early," Paul said, his eyes fixed on the blonde as she moved.

"Maybe she's just heading home after a night out?"

"Looks more like an advertisement to me," Paul said.

The timer ran out, and when the blonde deposited two more quarters to start the vac, nothing happened. She turned, saw me and my clean up gear, and looked me in the eye.

"Say, you work here? This machine just took my money."

"Won't take a moment," I said.

I unlocked the face of the vac and her nicked quarter tumbled onto the pavement. I closed the machine, deposited another quarter, and the vac roared to life.

"Thanks. These things suck pretty good."

She demonstrated the power of the vac by sucking three inches of her skirt into the hose. Then she smiled at us and slowly pulled her skirt from the vac. Paul and I stood by uneasily as she cleaned the rear seat of the Mustang.

I hadn't had any female attention since I had inherited Texas Pride, or really since my former girl friend, Pam, took a job teaching in Throckmorton. Pam wasn't the ordinary grad student. She was nearly thirty years old, just a couple of years younger than I, and had been divorced—no kids—before starting on the grad degree. She had been on the rodeo team in undergraduate school; that didn't seem unusual for someone who had grown up in Perryton in the far north Panhandle just a few miles from the Oklahoma and Kansas borders. She wrote her thesis on rodeo lit, a sort of compare-contrast analysis of how the rodeo settings promoted themes in Larry McMurtry's *Moving On* and Sara Bird's *Virgin of the Rodeo*. Pam was a born English major who read everything that fell her way from classics to trash and who just happened to be from cowboy world west Texas.

Truth was that I missed Pam a lot. I felt more than a little guilty about letting her get away without a fight. But what could I have promised her? A low paying teaching position in some Oklahoma community college? And as Tim had reminded me at my tenure meeting, anyone with any self respect would "rather eat wood" than sink to junior college teaching. I didn't even have enough, when Pam and I were together, to make a down payment on a ring, and I doubt that she would have accepted my proposal. She was marriage shy after her first short, failed attempt at matrimony. So I had stood, silently, as she explained that since she had finished the Master's, she had taken a job at the high school in Throckmorton. There was talk of starting, someday, a high school rodeo club.

I knew something about Throckmorton because of my research on the literary Big Country. Throckmorton isn't much better that Oklahoma; it's one Allsup's and two small grocery stores away from being a ghost town three hours west of Fort Worth. I always knew I was in west Texas when I spotted an Allsup's. Allsup's is a family owned chain of convenience store gas stations that had its beginnings in New Mexico. In places like Throckmorton, the Allsup's is where you get coffee with your pals, buy fuel, fast food, and household supplies. In addition to the 24/7 Allsup's, Throckmorton was blessed with two stores, Clint's and Coalson's, both on Minter. The problem with Throckmorton wasn't groceries. So long as there were no EMP events, the highways would remain open and the supply trucks would came through; there would be food in Throckmorton. The problem was alcohol, more exactly the lack of it. Throckmorton was a totally dry county. You could get beer in Seymour, in neighboring Baylor County, and you could get beer, wine, and liquor in Haskel. It was a bit more than a sixty mile round trip to either Seymour or Haskel from Throckmorton.

As a high school English teacher, Pam would be making more money than I had been earning at SEPSU, and it wouldn't have been fair to ask her to stay with me in my double wide on the outskirts of Grassland when she could be making a stab at a life and job. I imagined she would eventually find someone, and I prayed it would not be the high school football coach, even if he were the highest paid person in Throckmorton County. There were times when I even considered going to Throckmorton and making a case for myself since I had quit teaching and become a business owner, but I was always busy and never worked up enough courage to take on the drive.

The life of a self-serve car wash owner is an isolated life. I usually saw Lloyd or Gary for a few minutes each day, but sometimes a week would go by before I would run into Linda, the head of the clean up crew. I left Linda's pay, always an envelope stuffed full of five dollar bills, in a locked metal case that had once housed an air compressor for car tires. With the compressor gone, I had a safe secured by dual Abus locks. Linda had a key, and I would simply lock the weekly pay envelope in the safe for her to pick up when the crew did the four a.m. cleaning.

I didn't have much in common with my employees, and that was probably a good thing. I had learned the hard way with Gonzalo that trusting the help too much was a bad idea. As far as I could tell, my employees had absolutely no interest in end-of-the-world fiction, and it was a good guess that they didn't read poetry in their spare time. Gary, the mechanic, was a biker with grizzly bear buddies who looked like beer and meth were their main food groups. Lloyd, who checked my machines with painted quarters, never read anything except the sports page in the *Star-Telegram*. I feared that Lloyd, who was nearly seventy years old, would end up like Jake: dead on the lot from a sudden heart attack. Linda and Doyle, my clean up crew, had trouble understanding written instructions, and I'd fired Gonzalo after the forty-thousand-dollar tamales incident. I sometimes considered taking a class at TCU or even applying for a part time job in the Writing Center, tutoring students, just so I could get a social life of sorts.

"Guess I better leave you to your duties," Paul said. He nodded toward the spaniel. "God knows I've got mine."

The woman finished vacuuming the car, replaced the hose in its holder, started the Mustang, and pulled slowly off the lot onto Cleburne Road.

The blonde in the Mustang seemed a bit upscale for a self serve-car wash hooker, but she was clearly looking for attention. Lots of hookups started at Texas Pride, so showing some skin was no big deal, but being as obvious as the Mustang blonde made me think she was, indeed, a prostitute.

There was a long history of prostitution in Fort Worth. Just over a hundred years back, Hell's Half Acre, the red-light zone where Butch Cassidy and his gang were photographed, thrived openly. As the West settled down, prostitution went underground. But, going east toward Stop Six, anyone could spot the hookers that lined Rosedale. Prostitutes would swing through the wash several times on a busy day, but most of the ladies that cruised Texas Pride and the other self-serves looked a bit rough around the edges. They reminded me of the prostitutes who haunt the giant truck stops out on the Interstates—sort of industrial grade sex workers.

Usually, I didn't bother asking the "ladies of the street" to leave unless they loitered blatantly or actually got out of their cars and directly solicited one of my customers. For the most part, the pros didn't need to hang around waiting for a trick. Most of the trade was an "understood" sort of deal; the Johns knew who the Janes were and vice versa by benefit of a glance. Occasionally, a desperate hooker would attempt to turn tricks on the lot, but for the most part that sort of thing happened deep into the night when I tried to avoid the car wash at all costs. Nothing short of an alarm call would get me to the car wash after dark. The bad guys were like vampires; they hated light.

Then there were the hookups, pickups, and make outs. One couple would meet at noon each Thursday and leave a car in a dry bay. A few hours later, they would return for the car, kiss, and go their separate ways. This had been going on as long as I had been in charge of the location. And since Texas Pride was just down the road from TCU, lots of college kids cleaned their cars at the wash. This sometimes made for an odd mix of customers: rich college kids washing expensive cars, young guys waxing their rides, and families from around Gordon Avenue cleaning up their junkers. The neighborhood dudes used the lot as a hookup location; it was cheaper than going to a bar, you could sip a beer, wax your ride, and flirt with the honeys that circulated on warm days. In fact, most of my customers were young guys, so I stocked condoms in the vending machine. They were high profit and very popular.

Every now and then I would surprise some young

couple getting a bit too frisky in the back seat of a car, and catching some fat guy clutching a porno mag in one hand and using the other to gratify himself with the hose-suction of my high-powered vacs was a regular event on rainy afternoons. Such was the nature of sex at the self serve car wash.

The blonde appeared early the next Sunday, just as I was locking the equipment room after checking the lot. Same car, same girl, same vac, but this time two young rednecks driving a white pickup got an eyeful of the Mustang girl. They were happy to see her. I slowly walked to my truck, wondering if the blonde would make a deal, but she simply finished vacuuming and hung the hose on its rack. The rednecks said something to her, but she ignored them and started walking across the lot to the change machine by the equipment room door. She stood at the machine a moment, mini skirt and cowboy boots and all, a ten dollar bill in her hand.

"Damn," she said, seeing the sign that the changer only took ones and fives.

I locked up my pickup and went to the changer.

"Not working?" I asked.

"You work here, don't you. Sign says only fives and ones." I gave her a five and five ones for the ten, and she got her change.

"You get an early start on the cleaning," I said, nodding to the Mustang. "Great car, by the way."

"Yeah. I love my car. Like to keep it up. You've got a good wash and I can swing by here after work."

"Yeah? What do you do?"

"I'm a dancer."

She reached into her purse and produced a card:

Tiffany Freelove
Star Light Club/Airport Freeway
Private Parties and Performances

"You should come see me sometime. I'm there every Saturday night, all night. That's why I come by so early on Sunday mornings."

She smiled and looked at me with ice blue eyes.

"When you visit, bring lots of fives. I'll make you glad you did."

Even though I had bundles of bills for tips, I was never one to frequent the strip joints. By the time Tiffany took the stage at the Star Light Club, I'd be knocked out by a Saturday at Texas Pride. The weekends were my busiest time, especially when the weather was good, so after work on Saturday I would count some coins for the changers, drink a few beers, get some supper and some sleep, and start all over again on Sunday morning. But now, Sunday mornings were a little more promising as I made it a habit to look out for Tiffany.

Sure enough, if the weather were good, Tiffany and the red Mustang would grace the lot. Goodness, I loved to watch that woman vac a car.

"How come you never come by the club, Leo?" she asked, reading the name tag on my Texas Pride work shirt. "Don't you ever get out for fun, or are you married or pussy whipped or something?"

The way she said *pussy whipped* made my broom droop.

"No. No. I mean, not married."

"We have private party rooms at the club, for lap dancing and all. I bet you get lonely here, dealing with these machines and all that money every day. For special friends

69

like you, I could do a massage with happy ending. Only two hundred. You probably got that much in fives all the time."

"Go on now. I got enough problems. Don't get me worked up."

I lifted my broom and began sweeping. Tiffany holstered the vac hose onto the vac and climbed into the red Mustang.

"Just think about it, Leo," she said, starting the car and flashing me a smile.

I watched as she pulled off the lot and headed north on Cleburne Road, toward downtown.

Tiffany was a temptress, that was certain, and likely she was as dangerous as Homer's Sirens. But her world and my world could never mix. I knew enough about strip club culture to realize that it was full folks who would love to separate me from my money. Nothing would be "free" with Tiffany Freelove.

One Sunday in late June, I pulled onto the lot just after a cloudless dawn brightened the wide Fort Worth sky. Dawn was the only cool time of day in a Texas summer. I could tell that Linda and the clean up crew had been by because there wasn't much trash blowing around. The lot was empty except for the red Mustang parked at its usual vac and a brown Buick Riviera parked at the next vac. There was no sign of Tiffany.

I got out of my truck and started for the equipment room. Then I heard her.

"No you fucking bastard. Leave me alone!"

I ran to the vac islands past the Mustang and into the alley that separated the deli from my lot and the animal hospital. A tall, thin white guy with stringy brown hair had

Tiffany pinned against the wire fence, one hand on her shoulder and the other on her right breast, and his pal, a musclebound skinhead with an earring and a bushy beard, was on the ground pawing through Tiffany's purse. They both wore jeans and white t-shirts, and I suspected their last long term address was in Huntsville. As far as I could tell they weren't armed.

"What's going on, fellows?" I said.

"Fuck you, shithead."

"My name's not shithead. Now just let the girl go and be gone."

The one on the ground dropped Tiffany's purse and stood up. He was plenty big with log-like biceps. His right arm was stamped with a tattoo, the number 14.

"We gonna mess you up first."

The big skinhead started toward me while his partner kept a hold on Tiffany.

"I'm going to tear you a new one, shithead."

I backed up fifty feet down the alley toward the lot, my eyes on the big man as he approached me. There was no one around, not even any traffic on Cleburne Road.

"Huntsville calling. Cops on the way now," I said, waving my phone in my left hand and pulling my shirt up with my right hand so that the giant could see me grab the butt of my Chief's Special.

That did the trick. The skinhead grunted and the tall one released Tiffany. They backed up and walked around me to get to the Riviera.

"You better watch your ass, shithead," the skinhead said to me as he started the Buick. "We know where to find you."

I kept a firm hand on the .38.

They left the lot with a screech of tires, heading south

71

toward I-20.

"Thanks," Tiffany said, brushing off her sun dress and picking her purse up from the ground. "I think they followed me from the club. They wanted the Mustang. And maybe me too."

"Sort of isolated out on the lot this early," I said.

"Did you really call the cops."

"No."

"Do you always carry a pistol?"

"Yes."

"They seemed friendly at first. I was in a good mood. Flirted with them a little. Then the big one grabbed my purse and next thing I knew the tall one was dragging me into the alley."

"I'm sorry," I said.

Tiffany checked the contents of her purse.

"Thank god they didn't get my phone," she said. "Didn't get anything because of you."

She gave me a quick kiss, got into her car, and slowly pulled off the lot.

And that was the last I saw of Tiffany Freelove.

Chapter 6
Lost and Found

There was a lot of lost and found at Texas Pride. Like Tiffany, people came and people went. There were lost persons, animals, and things aplenty. There were treasures aplenty, too. Everyday, valuable items ended up in the Texas Pride Dumpster. A sociology professor could make a career studying usable items that Americans toss away: good furniture, new clothing, tools. The American talent for wastefulness was just another part of the conspicuous consumption that characterized the national ethos. And just to prove the cliche´ that one man's trash is another man's treasure, a parade of scavengers went through the trash, looking for everything from aluminum cans to lost coins. At first, these scourgers irritated me, but I came to accept their presence as inevitable as that of the hookers and drug addicts who paid the lot a visit, and if the scavengers didn't strew a lot of trash about, I allowed them to conduct their searches unmolested. And people were always losing things in the vacs. Linda and Doyle, the clean-up crew, shoveled out the vac traps for free, keeping what they found in coins, bills, and jewels as their pay. In fact, they were glad that I had fired Gonzalo because they had split their vac take with him. Usually whatever was lost was never seen again, but sometimes items were recovered.

July was one of the hottest in Fort Worth's history, which made it one of the hottest in the history of the United States, and at first I thought the people in bay number one were just horsing around, spraying each other with cooling shots of rinse water. In the city, a self-serve car wash offers space and shade and water in the summer heat, sort of like an urban water park, and I had seen folks splash each other until they were soaked. But there were eight of them, all scruffy guys, four leaning against the brick wall and four lying on the concrete bay floor. I thought they were wearing swimming trunks and were washing an old work van, but as I climbed out of my truck and approached them, I saw that they were actually stripped down to their underwear. The van was an old Dodge the color of mud with *Last Chance Salvation Center* painted on its sides in large white letters.

A fully-clothed fellow who didn't look a whole lot better than the guys in their underwear deposited four quarters in the coin slot and took the wand in his hand. Before I could stop him, he turned the dial switch to "Wash" and begin hosing down his charges with hot soapy water dispensed at 1200 pounds pressure.

The high pressure spray startled the homeless fellows into sobriety: the ones leaning against the wall danced and jumped like they had been jolted with electricity, and the ones passed out on the bay floor came to and squirmed across the concrete like catfish out of water. One of the men sprang to his feet so quickly that his false teeth popped out of his open mouth, bounced against the concrete floor of the bay, slipped through the metal blades of the grill that covered the drain, and disappeared into the foul muck of grease, soap, dirt, and water that I called the "soup."

The homeless fellows were howling now that their caretaker was stripping off bits of their skin when he hit them too close with the high pressure wash. I stepped into the bay and switched the dial to "No-Spot Rinse," a low pressure cycle that delivered mineral free water as a final rinse that left cars spotless. The No-Spot feature was one reason why the Texas Pride location was beating out the competition, the Squirt, Wipe and Go wash just a few miles away.

"What are you trying to do to these guys," I asked the caretaker, "skin them alive? That's 1200 pounds of pressure on the soap cycle."

"I didn't realize," the fellow said as he continued to rinse off his now fully awake friends.

After the soap was off, the fellows moved out into the sun to dry, which didn't take long in the record heat. The temperature would probably top out at 105 or 106.

"You know, this equipment is really for cars, not people. You need to be more careful."

"Damn right," one of the guys said, surveying the welt on his arm where the high pressure soap had burnt him.

"Don't worry about it. At least they came clean."

"What about my teeth?" one of the fellows asked, pointing a finger at the pit, the soup.

"You're welcome to try to fish them out if you want. I doubt you'll want them even if you find them."

I knew that drunks often pissed and shit into the pits late at night and that the dopers often threw their used hypodermic needles into the soup to get rid of them. And more than a few used condoms spiced the broth.

The toothless fellow got down on his hands and knees and stared forlornly into the pit. He lifted the metal grill—it was chained to the concrete floor of the wash bay to keep the scavengers from stealing it and selling it for scrap metal—and pushed it aside. He jumped into the pit feet first and begin feeling the sludge with his toes. I was certain he would be

75

jabbed by a hypo needle, but instead he quickly found his teeth.

"Got them," he said, reaching down and grabbing the false teeth that he had clutched between his toes.

He climbed out of the pit, teeth in hand, and replaced the grill. A fresh, sour-sweet odor rose from the soup. I gagged and turned away.

The driver of the van deposited another dollar and turned the selector dial to "engine cleaner," a low pressure cycle. The toothless fellow held his teeth gingerly in his palmed hands as the driver rinsed them with degreaser. The thick muck of the soup melted from the teeth, leaving them gleaming and white. After rinsing his legs and the false teeth with the no spot cycle, the toothless fellow carefully fitted the teeth back into his mouth and smiled widely.

"There you are sir," he said. "Good as new."

They all piled back into the van and drove away, heading for downtown and the Last Chance Salvation Center.

It was easy to lose track of time at Texas Pride. The location was open 365 days a year, twenty-four hours a day. Weeks and months blended together, characterized only by some weather event or change of season. Then something would happen that would shock me out of routine and into the moment, like the time we found a "man down" in bay one.

The call woke me up at 5:30 a.m., too late to be an alarm but just the right time for Lloyd to have arrived at the location. Lloyd had worked three decades as a civilian employee of the Corps of Engineers. He was forever chewing on a half smoked cigar and talking about Fort Worth's favorite team, the TCU Horn Frogs. He had actually graduated from TCU decades ago and made it a point to be at every home football game.

Lloyd had suffered a minor nervous break down at the end of his career with the engineers, and in his retirement he was slowly going feral, hitting the bourbon a little earlier each day and putting on a bit of weight. But some of the old office discipline was still there, and he showed up at Texas Pride every day and took great care to test all the machines with red quarters. And I was pretty sure his wife ordered him to bathe because he never stank of anything except bourbon and cigars. At least once a week Lloyd threatened to turn in his keys because of the crime and dirt, but he could never bring himself to resign.

"Better get on up here," Lloyd said when I answered the phone. "We got a man down in bay one."

"Down?"

"Yeah. Down as in dead. The cops are on the way."

The police were there when I arrived. They had roped off the entire lot with yellow tape and four patrol cars blocked the entrances from the streets. I hoped that they wouldn't take too long and keep me shut down on a Saturday morning, my busiest time.

The cops huddled around a red Ford Taurus. It was a battered 1995 model that looked like it had been driven though hell and back. Lloyd walked over from one of the cop cars where he and an officer had been talking.

"Found him first thing when I got here," Lloyd told me, nodding toward the Taurus in bay one. "Looks like he took a wild last ride."

I introduced myself to the officer guarding the car. The name tag on her uniform read M. Garcia. The Taurus was occupied by a young fellow about the same age as my SEPSU students. He sat with blue eyes wide open, staring into infinity. He gripped the steering wheel with two frozen hands that looked like bird claws, the needle still in his vein, the tourniquet still wrapped around his arm.

I gagged and coughed.

"First one?" the officer asked.

Garcia was a battle-hardened forty year old whose long black hair, pinned up behind her cap, was already starting to grey. Her hand rested naturally on the butt of her holstered pistol.

"Yeah."

"It takes some getting used to."

"Yeah."

"Count yourself lucky. This one's not too messy, not like a murder or suicide with a gun shot wound. We'll have the car towed as soon as the medical examiners move the body. Might be a couple of hours."

Just then, Gary walked over from the vet's, where he had parked since the cops had blocked off the lot.

"Boy howdy!" Gary said.

He took off his "Here for a Good Time, Not a Long Time" ball cap in an act of automatic respect for the dead. Gary and his biker buddies were rough cut but they had a code of behavior.

"That kid went out hard core. I don't where they get such powerful stuff."

He put his cap back on an pulled at his beard a bit, giving the dead kid a long look.

"Probably heroin," Garcia said. "You work here?"

"This is Gary," I said. "He's our mechanic."

We all stared at the body a while longer. What is it about the face of the dead that makes you look and look and look?

"You got anything for me to fix here?" Gary finally asked.

"We're okay."

"Good, I got more water heater trouble at Squirt, Wipe and Go. Owen is busting a nut about it."

Gary walked back to his truck and I noticed that several potential customers had been turned back by the police at the driveways.

"Maybe I could open up a couple a bays on the other end of the wash?"

Officer Garcia shook her head and gave me a stern look.

"Not until we tow the car."

There was no point in arguing, so I nodded my acceptance.

God damn the pusher man!

The kid lost his life at Texas Pride; Gene lost his mind. I am pretty certain it was because of the ayahuasca even though Gene tried to blame it on the curse of the irritable Tibetan bowl.

As was my custom in the summer, I got an especially early start one morning because I wanted to rob the safes before the heat set in, as it was sure to do. I recognized Gene's car, a 2010 white Nissan Altima, even before I got out of my truck.

Gene was sprawled, wide-mouth and snoring into his beard, in the fully reclined front seat. He was wearing a rumpled long sleeve white shirt and blue jeans and no shoes. I shook him by the shoulder.

"Gene. Hey. Gene. Come on buddy."

He blinked his eyes and slowly came to.

"Leo? What the hell!"

He jolted straight up in the seat.

"Bastards. They got it all. Keys, phone, wallet. Shit, they even took my Nike Flyknits," he said, realizing that he was barefooted. "And damn, they took the cursed bowl. They'll regret that."

Gene got out of the car and began looking around the bay, hoping that he would find his things.

"What happened? What were you doing up here in the middle of the night?"

Gene searched the back seat of the Altima, without success.

"It's a long story. I did an ayahuasca ceremony in Arlington last night. I took the cursed bowl with me because I planned to dump it in the Trinity on my way back home. Driving back from the ceremony I started to have some trouble. I had come in on I-30, and I was cruising down Forest Park. I wanted to stop at one of the parking lots on the bike trail and toss the bowl into the river. But every time I started to pull over, I felt dizzy, like I wasn't in control of the car. I thought I was going to throw up. I don't know. I needed some place safe, so I kept driving until I pulled off at your car wash."

That made sense to me. I figured about ten percent of Tarrant County had puked at Texas Pride one time or another.

"Ayahuasca ceremony?"

"Yeah, like the ones I plan to have in Big Bend. But they took it all."

"Who took what?" I asked.

"Robbers. They took my keys, my phone, my money from the ceremony. They even took the Tibetan bowl. They will be sorry for that. That bowl only brings its owner bad luck. This is a warning to me. A warning."

"Man, you just passed out after a rough night and someone lifted your stuff. You're lucky they didn't just push you out on the lot and take the car. This is a tough place."

"No, no," Gene said, running his fingers through his beard. "It's the curse of the bowl. You've got to help me. Take me to my house. I'll get my other keys."

So I ferried Gene back to his place. He didn't say a word until I pulled into the drive.

"Can you run me back to the lot for my car."

"Sure."

I followed him around the side of the house, where he retrieved a spare key from under a rock in the flower bed. Gene unlocked his back door and we went inside.

I was immediately stricken by the skunk smell of his drying marijuana which was hung upside down from the ceiling in one of the back rooms.

I drove Gene back to the Texas Pride lot where he jumped into the Nissan and started the engine.

"I was warned," Gene said. "I'll have to leave town now. Got to get to the desert."

"Come on, man. There aren't any spirits chasing you."

"When they discover the curse of the bowl, they will come for me."

"Really, Gene. You need to lay off the ayahuasca for a while."

Gene looked around as if he expected to see a ghost appear in each bay, then he shot me a "you're a bleeping idiot" look and pulled off the lot.

About a week later, Gene came by the house with a grocery sack full of dried bud.

"I want you to have these for helping me," Gene said.

He didn't look too good. Dark circles had formed around his eyes.

"The spirits are still troubled. It's clear I need to leave. I selling the house and heading for Terlingua Ranch."

"You don't have to leave, Gene. There's nothing chasing you out of town."

"I'm sorry you don't understand. You're still seeing only the surface reality. I'm being told to go. It's for the best. I've been planning on this move a long time. Now is the time to act."

Gene shook my hand and walked away. The next day, he left with his Nissan packed full of boxes and clothes, and the next week a realtor placed a *For Sale* sign in his yard. And that's how I lost Gene.

Chapter 7
A Girlfriend and Some Cowboy Poetry

I settled into my celibate routine and concentrated on banking and keeping the equipment running. I continued to have some regrets about Pam. She was truly queen of the rodeo. I kept telling myself that things had worked out for the best, but I really missed her. Pam was smart as well as being attractive in an athletic sort of way. It took some serious thigh muscles to stay on a horse in a barrel race. We had been together over a year when Pam broke it off to take a job teaching high school in Throckmorton. And I was happy for her. She was a good student, and I knew she would make a fine teacher, but I could imagine her marrying some simpleton west Texas football coach, and that troubled me. Pam was too good for me and much too good to spend her life at Friday night games with some drooling jock who would use her as a breeding machine. But, it was Throckmorton, so she might meet a millionaire rancher and do fine.

It was early September when I spotted a familiar looking car in one of the dry bays. It was a light blue, 2002 Crown Victoria that I knew from Grassland, except now the car wore a *Throckmorton Greyhounds* bumper sticker. The car belonged to Pam. The Crown Victoria was all that she took from her marriage; her husband, a fellow named Sam whom I had never met, had owned a car lot in Amarillo. I knew that the divorce and failed marriage had been rough on Pam because she never said much about it. And there she was, dressed in a respectable teacher top and skirt but wearing running shoes. She was just about to drop two quarters into the vac when I walked up.

"Don't waste your money on that machine," I said.

Pam turned to me in surprise.

"Leonard?"

"What are you doing at my Texas Pride Car Wash?"

"I heard you quit to work in some family business," Pam said. "But I never expected something like this."

She waved the vac hose around as if to illustrate the scope of the problem.

"I inherited it from my uncle," I said. "It's hard, dirty work but I'm making good money. Cleaning up, as we say."

Pam smiled, the same smile I had come to love over the course of a cold Panhandle winter in Grassland.

"You're sort of dressed up for car washing."

"I'm in town for a conference," Pam said. "One of my students won a poetry contest, and he and his parents are here for the awards this afternoon. I wanted to vac because I'm taking them to lunch."

"Here, let me."

I deposited coins in the vac and cleaned the front and rear seats and floorboards of the Crown Victoria. Pam had kept the car in good shape over the years, though it was a gas drinking V-8 and she could probably afford something newer on her teaching salary. I often thought she kept the car as a reminder of her past and her former husband, but if that were a good or bad thing I wasn't sure. Pam never said much about the marriage except that she and Sam were too young to know what they were doing. I knew the feeling well. I finished and hung the vac hose on the machine.

"So, your student wins a contest your first year on the job. How is the job, anyway?"

"I love teaching, and Throckmorton's not so bad. It's a 1A school, six man football. The kids are a lot like those in the Perryton."

"Yeah, the Greyhounds," I pointed to the bumper sticker. "Is the department okay?"

"We don't have departments," Pam laughed. "We're too small. It's just me and a few other teachers and the principal. Throckmorton is a tiny town with two markets and an Allsup's. I usually go to Graham or Haskell once a week for groceries and white wine. Throckmorton is a totally dry county, you know."

"Yeah. I was there doing research a couple of years back."

"Oh. I remember. The Literary Big Country article. Anyway, once a month or so I drive to Fort Worth to go to a restaurant and Central Market. It's just 270 miles round trip. Nothing, really, compared to driving in far west Texas. Anyway, Andy, my student, won first prize in the cowboy poetry contest. Part of the Red Steagall Cowboy Gathering. Tim Collard, Dr. Collard, is going to be there. He judged the contest, you know."

"Really. Good old Tim. I wonder how that search for my job went?"

"I don't stay in touch with the English department at SEPSU much," Pam said. "Anyway, I'm going to the awards ceremony this afternoon, and then Andy and his parents are going back to Throckmorton, but I'm staying over. Got a room at the Courtyard on University."

"Really. A room at the Courtyard."

"Don't suppose you'd like to escort me to the program?"

Naturally, I was as excited as a Throckmorton senior looking forward to a hot date. And I still loved Pam, no matter what happened. I didn't mind that she tended to talk a lot about horses and rodeos, and she didn't mind my specialization in post-apocalyptic fiction; the topics sort of fit together since we would all be riding horses after the EMP. She would tell me about Tex, her favorite horse, and how she would have never slid from the saddle if she had been riding Tex the night of the accident. Of course the accident had happened more than ten years back, when Tex was just a twinkle in a mare's eye. I had heard the accident story a dozen times, most often when Pam was moving from Chardonnay number three to Chardonnay number four.

"We were at San Angelo, Angelo State, early fall my senior year. It had been a long drive down from Stephenville, and we were all tired even before the events started. I was on a black mare named Kidd, a good horse that I'd ridden since high school, fast on the start up and well spirited. We crossed the eye on the barrels and Kidd was running fine. I was trying to shave six seconds off the run, and I must have pushed her too hard coming around the second barrel."

Pam would take a sip of wine and stare thoughtfully into her glass.

"Anyway, Kidd went into a slide and threw me. Next thing I know I'm on the ground with my leg twisted up under me. That was that. Lot's of time to read after that."

And she would listen with interest, or at least feigned interest (which is usually the best you can hope for in a committed relationship) as I summarized the most recent EMP novel that I had discovered.

There are many post apocalyptic scenarios: super plagues, asteroid collision, volcanic eruption, weather change, economic collapse, and nuclear war, just to name a few. EMP was my speciality because to me it seemed to be the most likely of the scenarios to occur. EMP stands for *electromagnetic pulse*. EMP events are caused by solar flares, such as in the case of the famous Carrington Event in 1859, which knocked out telegram systems in Europe and the US, or by nuclear explosion as demonstrated by the Starfish Prime test in 1962. In that test, the United States detonated a 1.44 megaton warhead 250 miles into space over the south Pacific. The explosion caused a "pulse" that blew out telephones and lights in Hawaii. A 1.44 megaton warhead is small compared to what is out there these days. In most of the EMP novels, terrorists, North Koreans, or some rouge Middle Eastern actors explode an atomic device above Kansas, destroying the electric grid. Experts estimate that about ninety percent of the US population would die of violence, starvation, and disease within a year of the EMP event. In a lot of these narratives, the loss of population combined with intact resources such as the immense corn and wheat belts of the mid west would invite invasion, usually by Chinese or UN troops.

Many of the EMP narratives are quest stories, adventures about searching for lost family after the power goes out forever. Often, the hero is a exceptionally fit ex Ranger, a veteran of the wars in the "sand box," who is attending a business conference far from his home when the EMP hits, separating our hero from his family. Since the EMP has destroyed nearly all motorized transportation, our protagonist must find some alternative means of making it home: foot, bicycle, horseback, hot air balloon, or working antique car. (A horse like Tex would be handy to have around in the case of an EMP attack.) In one story the characters float rafts down the Missouri River to reach St. Louis. And there are always the preppers who have hoarded guns, ammo, and freeze-dried food. Throw in some cannibal bad guys or murderous bikers and you've got a plot.

The EMP issue had become more publicized recently due to North Korea's Kim Jong-un and his missile program. Since I was obsessed with the topic, I expected Kim to launch an EMP attack on the United States at any moment. I had held this expectation for several years, and I often blamed my writer's block on this obsession. What was the point of writing an academic book that few people would read when the EMP could hit at any moment? I began to have increased respect for Jake and Sue and my parents who had lived through the Cold War "Duck and Cover" years. How had they gone on, year after year–working, planning, playing–while under the cloud of end-times war? And in my wildest dreams, dreams that I hadn't even shared with Pam, I imagined the two of us retreating post-EMP attack to our hidden "bug out" ranch in the Palo Pinto Mountains west of Fort Worth. A cabin with a spring and a couple year's supply of food, booze, and fuel–not to mention firearms and ammo–would be enough. Tex could graze on the native grasses. Such is the stuff of EMP dreams.

I spent the afternoon digging my dress shirt, slacks, and sports coat out of the closest and dusting off a pair of nearly new cowboy boots–bought two years earlier to celebrate the publication of one of Tim's cowboy poetry books. I had heard about the Steagall Cowboy Gathering but had never attended. It was an annual festival held in the historic Fort Worth Stockyards. As in previous years, the program was a mix of country music, cowboy poetry, and chuck wagon cookery. It seemed like a pretty good combination if you could tolerate cowboy poetry.

I drove to the Stockyards and parked on the Billy Bob's lot where I had agreed to meet Pam. The tourists were already pouring out of Billy Bob's; there were morning and afternoon tours of the enormous dance hall that frequently hosted country music legends such as Willie Nelson. Within minutes, Pam pulled up in the Crown Victoria, followed by a white Ford F-150 duel cab pickup. A tall, skinny high school boy with short black hair and brown eyes got out of the backseat of the truck: Andy, the cowboy poet. His parents, the father dressed in boots, pressed jeans, white shirt and white hat; the mother wearing a black Western-style pants suit and cowboy boots, climbed down from the cab. Pam made the introductions, gave us our tickets, and we walked to the Stockyards coliseum where the poetry reading would take place.

"Pam tells me that you used to be a college professor."

"That's right," I told Andy's mother. "Pam was once a grad student of mine out in Grassland, at South East Panhandle State University. We even get students from Throckmorton every now and then."

"You don't teach now?"

"No, I inherited a business from my uncle. A coin op car wash on Cleburne Road. It's been a change of pace for sure."

The streets siding the coliseum were staged for music, and smoke curled from the pit fires in front of a gaggle of chuck wagons tended by performer cowboys dressed in chaps and spurred boots. People lined Exchange Avenue, getting ready for the longhorn cattle drive, a twice a day event in which a dozen long-horned cattle were escorted down Exchange by cowboys on horseback.

We were a few minutes late—the lights in the auditorium were dimmed—and Andy had to report backstage to prepare for his reading. Pam, the parents, and I settled into seats. On stage, Tim Collard, chair of the English Department at South East Panhandle State University, stood behind a podium and tapped the mic—thump, thump, thump—to make sure it was working. He wore his usual cowboy garb: pressed blue jeans, white shirt with mother-of-pearl buttons, a turquoise bolo, and black Stetson. White and black and blue as in jeans seemed to be favorite cowboy colors.

"Ladies and gentlemen," Tim said, his too familiar voice dragging me back to SEPSU and my days in the English Department, "welcome to the annual Red Steagall Cowboy Gathering, Music Festival, and Poetry Reading. I'm Dr. Tim Collard, and I direct the English Department at South East Panhandle State University in Grassland, just on the edge of the Cap Rock—real cowboy territory. I'm the author of several books of cowboy poems, including my most recent, *When Cows Cry*, on sale out front, and it's my pleasure tonight to introduce you to some of the most outstanding young cowboy poets in the nation. We'll even get to hear our winning cowboy poet read the winning cowboy poem. All the student poems are collected in an chapbook, *Voices from the Young West*, also available out front, for free, thanks to the generosity of the Red Steagall Foundation for the Advancement of Cowboy Culture."

There was a round of polite applause.

"Our contest was open to all upper school students in the 'cowboy' counties to the west of Fort Worth. Our winners are young men and women who long for and recall the life of the ranch and the cowboy, a nearly forgotten way of life, on the plains and arroyos where a little more than a century ago herds of buffalo trod and the Comanche rode. Though we will only have time to hear the winning poem, all the poems we honor today are included in *Voices from the Young West*, and they all share an ethos that places them with the finest of cowboy poetry: a love of the land and family and horses, a love of freedom and country and God."

The mention of God and country brought a more

enthusiastic applause. Then Tim proceeded to call the names of twenty some students, each of whom walked across the stage (to the accompaniment of parental applause) and shook hands with Tim when he handed them their award checks.

"Don't forget to pick up a copy of the chapbook and take the time to read the poems by these fine young ladies and gentlemen, and why not buy a copy of *When Cows Cry*, too," Tim continued. "It makes a great gift, and I know you'll enjoy both books. And now, it's my pleasure to present our winning cowboy poet and poem for this year's Red Steagall Cowboy Gathering. His name is Andy Wilson, he's from Throckmorton, on the edge of the Big Country, and he's here today with his parents Jim and Lynda Wilson, and his teacher in Throckmotorn, Pam Nixon, a SEPSU graduate by the way, who encouraged Andy to enter this contest. Let's welcome Andy Wilson who will read his winning poem: "Last Roundup.""

Andy approached the podium, nodded to Tim and to the audience, took a sip of water from the bottle he carried, and began to read his poem in a steady, measured voice:

Last Roundup
A cowboy's days and nights
on the sun-struck plains
teach to him God's grace and might.
The call of the cattle promise tomorrow's gains,
but beyond the dying embers of a campfire
the evening mists linger, like spirits, across the gully,
reminding the cowboys when they retire
that this worldly cattle drive is just a folly.
As they spread their bedrolls out besides their saddles,
the full moon sears the darkening sky,
silence descends upon the lowing cattle,

while the prairie winds begin to die.
In the sky above the stars spin and inspire—
to heaven's last roundup a cowboy should aspire.

There was yet more applause. Tim shook Andy's hand and delivered the prize.

"Ladies and gentlemen, join me in congratulating Andy Wilson of Throckmorton for his fine poem and let's thank Red Steagall for this $500 check for best poem at this year's gathering."

The crowd began to filter out of the auditorium.

"I'm impressed," I said. "The metrics need a little work, but it's an English sonnet, and the theme is serious."

"I taught the class sonnets," Pam said. "English one week and Italian the next."

"And Andy is a very religious boy," Mrs. Wilson added. "He read that poem last week in Sunday school."

"He wants to be a preacher some day," Mr. Wilson said.

The Wilsons and Pam and I lingered at the book sales table while we waited for Andy. Mrs. Wilson had collected a half dozen copies of *Voices from the Young West* to give to her fellow church ladies in Throckmorton, and Mr. Wilson cautiously fingered a copy of Tim's latest book, *When Cows Cry,* published by Ghost Town Press and on special sale at the cowboy gathering for just ten dollars. Tim's book was a thin paperback with the face of a longhorn on the cover, a single tear drop falling from the longhorn's large brown eye. I glanced at the blurbs on the back:

"These one hundred poems, each in the voice of a different longhorn on a cattle drive, bring a fresh perspective to the genre," said the critic from *Cowboy Poetry Today.*

"Puts the cow back into cowboy poetry" noted

Western Verse.

And, according to *Modern Ranch Life*, "Tim Collard has given us the *Spoon River Anthology* of cowboy poetry."

Tim suddenly appeared by Mr. Wilson's side.

"I'd gladly autograph that copy," Tim said "You must be Andy's father. He's got a lot of talent. You should be very proud of him."

"Thanks. We are proud of Andy. But I don't read much poetry out on the ranch."

Mr. Wilson carefully placed the copy of *When Cows Cry* back on the table.

"Why, Leonard. My goodness," Tim said, shaking my hand like he had just sold me a bum horse. "Look at you. I heard you were in Fort Worth, doing something. What was it? Washing cars? That's great, Leonard. It's good you found something using your hands, something that suits you better."

I nodded. "Congrats on the new book. Looks like a winner."

"Yes, hopefully my breakthrough volume. I'd like to get a slot on the big money cowboy poetry reading circuit."

Andy came from the backstage area and stood silently beside his parents.

"Really liked the poem," I said. "A sonnet is a tough form."

"Thank you."

I picked up a copy of *When Cows Cry* and handed it to Tim.

"I'll take one of these, but autograph it to Andy, our winning poet."

"Why sure," Tim said.

He whipped a pen from his shirt pocket, turned to the title page of his book, and quickly inscribed the volume. He gave the book to Andy, and I gave Tim a couple of fives. As usual, I had about fifty of them in my wallet.

"Thank you both," Andy said.

He was clearly the polite, quiet type of cowboy poet.

"Andy and his folks are heading back to Throck-morton," Pam said. "Would you want to join us for dinner?"

I held my breath. Pam had forgotten or was oblivious to the hostility between me and Tim.

"Well now that's really thoughtful," Tim said. "But I'll have to pass on the invitation. I'm heading over to the Cowgirl Museum to check out the archives. I hear they are in possession of a rare cowgirl poem written by Georgia O'Keeffe. Lines written on the occasion of the arrival of the train in Canyon, or something like that. At least that's the rumor."

Pam laughed nervously.

"Have a great time," I said.

"Yes." Tim said, as we walked out onto Exchange Avenue. "And good luck to you, Leonard. I mean that. I know things didn't work out at SEPSU like you wanted, but it wasn't personal."

"No," I said. "Not personal."

"And you're milking a 'cash cow' now for sure."

"Maybe I'll write a cash cow poem about it."

Tim smiled and turned away, walking down Exchange. We headed back to the parking lot of Billy Bob's.

"What did he write in your book?" Andy's mother asked.

Andy flipped open the book to the title page and read the inscription.

"It says 'Congratulations and good luck with all your cowboy poems. Tim Collard, Red Steagall Cowboy Gathering, Fort Worth, Texas.'"

"That's sweet," Mrs. Wilson said. "Thanks for making

him enter the contest. And it was nice meeting you, too."

"Same here," I said. "Good to meet you folks."

The Wilsons got into their pickup and waved as they drove off, leaving me and Pam standing in the parking lot.

"Well," Pam said, taking my hand. "What now, cowboy? Want to go for a ride?"

Chapter 8
Magic Coins

The months since Pam and I had been apart seemed not to exist as we fell back into easy familiarity. Pam confessed that life in Throckmotorn had been lonely and that sometimes she dreamed of us as we were in the past, snuggled up in my double wide against a Panhandle winter. Before long, we were even talking marriage, but Pam was in no hurry to make things legal. Logistics were awkward, what with my having to be at Texas Pride every day and Pam having to teach in Throckmorton. She made it clear that she didn't intend to give up her teaching job to move to Fort Worth. Besides, Pam was still a little marriage shy as a result of her first foray into matrimony.

Throckmorton was home to six hundred people, not a place where my overnight, unmarried visits with the English teacher would go unnoticed. Sometimes we would meet in Graham, and sometimes Pam would drive into Fort Worth for the weekend. Occasionally, she would ride with me when I checked out the Texas Pride location. When Pam was around, I tried to make the visits quick ones; no need wasting time at Texas Pride on those days. Sometimes a couple of weeks would pass before we could arrange a meeting, especially when Pam would drive to Perryton in the far north Panhandle to visit her family and her horse. Her father worked for the county and her mother was some sort of a nurse. They had a thousand acre place with a barn where Pam kept Tex. I looked forward to meeting them sometime, but I had no idea when that would be. But even though we couldn't be together every day, I knew that Pam and I were lucky, and I wondered if we would have ever found each other again if not for Texas Pride.

I was dreaming of Pam's next visit to Fort Worth when the Magic Man appeared. I was cleaning up the lot–picking up the broken beer bottles and the soiled diapers–sorting through the urban refuse of another day. It was late October, but the temperature had shot up to ninety. The Magic Man was muscular, but not too tall. He wore baggy pants that sagged low on his butt, and he had shed his shirt because of the heat. His upper body was covered with tattoos: gang markings, women's names and odd designs that resembled abstract art. On his right arm was a large tattoo of a hammer. The tattoos seemed to move and swarm beneath the sweat that glazed his chest.

"Hey," he demanded, "you work here?"

No, I thought, I'm sweeping used diapers off of this stinking lot just for fun. But I put on my best "mentally challenged" smile and said, "Yeap, how can I help yee?"

"My coin, man. I lost my magic coin. I want it back."

He pointed to one of the wash bays, and I realized that the man had deposited his "magic coin" into the slot that dropped quarters into a bay safe.

"What kind of coin is it?"

"Like a quarter, man, but gold. There's a picture of a naked girl on it. Titty side reads 'Heads I Win.' Ass side reads 'Tails You Lose.' It was a couple of weeks ago I lost it here."

Another case of lost and found at Texas Pride. I knew then that I would probably never locate the coin. Either it was buried beneath all the quarters I needed to count or it had slipped through the counting machine and been deposited in a thousand-dollar bag that, by now, would be sitting in the Federal Reserve Bank in Dallas.

"It's important I get my coin back," the tattooed man said, his eyes shifting to a car parked in one of the drying bays.

It was a primer-blotched Impala with two gangsters hanging onto the doors. The gang members glared at me.

"I just do the clean up. But I can ask the owner if he found any coin like yours. Can you leave a number?"

"Fuck no, I'm not leaving no fucking number you retardo. You tell your dude that Hammer, that's me, wants his coin back. The coin, man. It stands for our magic."

"I get it. Heads I win, and tails you lose."

"We never lose," Hammer said, giving me the evil eye as he walked back to the Chevy and joined his friends.

The gangsters stared hard at me as the car pulled off the lot and turned toward downtown on Cleburne Road.

I knew what sort of coin the man was talking about. Every few months I would find one mixed in with the quarters. The coin was a token, the kind that guys fed to the machines at the video-sex shops. Usually, I tossed these porno coins into the pits with the other slugs people used to cheat the equipment. But I hadn't seen any porno coins for a long time because—in a raid that was the subject of an ongoing lawsuit—Tarrant County's sheriff had shut down most of the X-rated video parlors.

The Magic Man wasn't the first to lose something at the wash. At least once a week someone lost, or thought he lost, a precious ring in one of the vacs. Then I would have to unlock the vac trap and shovel through the accumulated dust and filth in search of a lost treasure that, more often than not, would never be found. One time a fellow from the Philippines had accidentally deposited a New York subway token in the coin slot. The man begged me to look for it, saying it was his good luck charm, the first thing he had gotten when he came to America. I emptied the safe and found the man's token. But that had been easy. The subway token had only been in the vault a few minutes when the man had asked for it back. It was unlikely that I could find a coin that had been deposited weeks ago.

"Magic coin my ass," I mumbled to myself as the gangsters drove away.

Despite my liberal arts background, I had never put much credence in myth or magic. I was a Naturalist; I thought nature, heredity, and luck determined most everything about our lives. I believed in science not only because I believed in the EMP threat but also because of what I saw every day. I got up every morning, went to work, and put my faith in electricity, physics, and mechanics—all the things that kept the machines at the car wash moving, pumping, turning. Magic and myth sometimes worked in literature, but not, I thought, in reality. As much as I might like to, I couldn't wave a juju, grigri, fetish, amulet, or talisman over a broken pump and expect it to repair itself. I couldn't blow some cigarette smoke out my nose, recite an incantation, wave my arms around and expect a broken hose to seal its wound. No, machines did not work that way, and neither did the world, at least not the world of the Texas Pride Car Wash.

And although the magic coin man looked pretty wild in his baggy gang pants and his illustrated-man tattoos, he was not that unusual. He was just another one of the lost souls I encountered at the car wash from time to time: the stripper I rescued from gangsters, the deranged man who had threatened me with a long knife, the crack cocaine addicts pleading for coins, the occasional prostitutes, the stream of hobos, bums, drunks and confused persons. Car wash life was the street life, and anything could happen on the street.

I finished cleaning up the lot, set the alarm, locked the barred doors that protected the equipment room and bill changers, and drove home to the house in Westcliff.

The last time Pam had visited, she had noticed the place could use a little work, but I explained that I didn't want to look too prosperous. The gray paint was faded inside and out, the yard needed mowing, and the burglar bars were rusting away. I was still waiting for the repair of the roof since the May hail storm. It would take a long time to replace all the roofs that the storm destroyed. There was a handgun in each room, a shotgun behind the front door, and thousands of dollars in quarters stacked up in my "office." I hadn't felt like banking since Pam's last visit. I always got a little blue when I had to face lonely time without her. It was possible, I thought as I eyed all those buckets of uncounted quarters, that the "magic" coin was still there.

I fixed some supper, counted enough coin to stock the changers the next day, took a shower, turned on the TV, and fell asleep after drinking a beer. I had completely forgotten Hammer and his magic coin.

Hammer hadn't forgotten. He was at the lot—with his two buddies—the next afternoon, waiting for me to arrive in my old pickup. Although I had plenty of money, I drove Jake's old Ford truck, dressed in rags, and acted like a "retardo" to keep the customers from thinking it would be worth their while to mug me. This ruse had worked for my uncle Jake and it had worked for me, but I still carried a .32 auto in my pocket, just in case.

It was another scorcher, and the Magic Man was shirtless; his tattoos swam under a glaze of sweat as he spoke.

"Find my coin, man."

I sensed a threat.

"I asked about it," I said, glancing at the car and the gangsters who were eyeing me. "But I don't think the owner can find it."

The Magic Man just stared at me for a moment as if he were considering what to do next.

"You tell that guy Hammer needs to talk to him. He had better give me back my coin. It's my magic, our symbol."

"Well, I can ask again, that's all I can do."

"You tell him to give me back my coin or there will be trouble. You don't mess with Hammer."

Hammer turned and walked to his car; he and his friends talked a moment and then sped away with a squealing of tires. I noticed that the rear window of the Impala had etching on it: "Heads I Win. Tails You Lose."

At home that evening, after I satisfied my thirst with a tall brew, I began counting coins. Counting was a chore that was never really completed–and I was glad of that–because it meant that business was steady. The money had stacked up for weeks, but I was tired, and I only ran a couple of buckets through the counting machine, looking all the while for the "magic" coin. There was an occasional slug and several quarters with holes drilled through them, a vain attempt to cheat the machines by attaching a string or wire to the quarter, but there were no "magic" coins, no coins with naked women on them.

"To hell with the Magic Man and the coin with the naked girl."

I bagged another thousand in quarters.

"Do you know about magic?" Hammer demanded. "If

the magic goes bad, or if you lose your honor, things go wrong."

I listened patiently; what else could I do? The Magic Man came by every afternoon and waited, with his unsavory pals, so he could ask again about the "magic" coin.

"I don't think we're going to find your coin," I said. "It's probably in the bank by now."

"Listen, if my magic changes, so does yours," Hammer said, his tattoos gleaming purple in the sunlight.

I took a rag from my back pocket and wiped the sweat from my face.

"Look fellow. I don't want trouble. If you think a machine cheated you, I can give you a refund."

Hammer snorted and spit and I could see the anger rise in his eyes. Then he turned and joined his friends who were waiting near the Chevy. The gangsters consulted a minute, then climbed into their car and sped down the street.

"Crazy thugs," I thought, letting my hand slide into my right front pants pocket where I carried the .32 auto. The fully loaded gun—eight shots of hollow-pointed power resting behind a double-action trigger—made me feel better. That was magic okay. I decided that from then on I would also carry a .38 revolver or a Glock 26 in a waist-band holster, as if two pistols were the charms needed to protect me against the curse of a mad, "magic" man. I locked up the door to the equipment room and went home, sure that the gangsters would destroy something that night.

Much to my surprise when I returned the next morning, the wash seemed undamaged: no graffiti, no cut hoses, no smashed vending machines. But inside the equipment room the float valve on the hot-water holding tank had broken; three inches of water flooded the floor.

For a moment I just looked at the flooded equipment room and considered how easy it would be to make a mistake, to accidentally touch one of the 220 wires while standing ankle-deep in water. So I stepped back, used the wooden handle of a broom to clear the debris from the floor drain, and watched the flood recede.

The Magic Man did not appear that day. The temperature approached ninety degrees again. It was the fifty-third day in a row without rain.

The next morning, nothing was destroyed at the lot. There wasn't even any gang graffiti to indicate that Hammer and his buddies were interested in the place. But mechanical problems seemed to pop up everywhere: two vac motors down, a busted low pressure pump on the tire cleaner, strange wiring problems that took forever to trace. It was as if the car wash gods were angry.

"Must be that curse the Magic Man put on me," I said, talking to myself.

The problems were, no doubt, related to stress and normal fatigue. After all, in the summer months, temperatures inside the equipment room could reach 130 degrees Fahrenheit and in the winters drop as low as 40 degrees, even with the space heater running. That sort of range, combined with the high humidity that came with softening, heating, and pumping thousands of gallons of water, wore down everything. There was nothing magic about it. No, there would be no magic, thank you, only electricity, physics, and sweat. That's what really keeps the world going, no matter what Gene and the New Age shamans or Tim Collard and the Postmodern English professors might claim; no matter what Hammer, with his gang buddies, his "magic coin," and his swarming tattoos might think. Back at SEPSU, I was the Naturalist in the English department. I believed that we live, we work, we die, and if we're a little bit fortunate because of "luck" or "fate" or "chance," we love a little before we die. Nothing very magical in that, just the normal course of human existence. I methodically repaired each vac and fixed the low-pressure pump. Even though it was October, the heat was straight out of hell.

Nearly every day, Paul and I talked through the wire threads of his fence. Paul, the vet, had gained a few pounds in the recent months. He had a shock of thick brown hair that always needed trimming. He had treated Jake's hound Dutch from the day that my aunt Sue and uncle Jake had found the poor, abandoned pup at the lot until the day that Dutch had to be put down. Paul was the hardest working man I ever met. I could count on him to check on his animal patients every day, just like I checked on my machines.

"How's the car wash world going?" he asked me one morning while I was sweeping up and he was walking a bulldog.

"Heat's killing me," I said. "Can you believe it's October?"

"Yeah, and tough on animals, too. The charity shelter's AC went out last night. All the animals had to be farmed out to temp locations. Me and some other vets are raising money for repairs. Sure would like to get that AC fixed on Monday."

"Count me in for a hundred in fives," I said.

Paul laughed and allowed the bulldog to pull him back into the animal hospital.

That casual promise of a hundred in fives was one of those acts of fate that proved the validity, at least to me, of Naturalism. Of course, I could entertain students with lectures about Naturalistic stories ("The Horse Dealer's Daughter") or novels (*McTeague*) but sometimes it is difficult to recognize Naturalism in our own affairs because we like to think we are in charge of our lives. Pretending to be in control of things is nothing more than a convenient lie that helps keep us sane, but sometimes something, some fateful thing, happens, and everything is changed forever. It was chance that my uncle Jake left me the Texas Pride Car Wash. It was chance that Pam visited my car wash while I was there. It was chance that the air conditioning at the animal shelter failed, chance that Paul mentioned the event to me, and chance that I promised to make a contribution. After talking with Paul, I went straight to my home office and counted out five hundred in fives, more than I had promised but still money I would never miss as I had discovered the closet full of fives that Jake had assembled. The afternoon was miserable hot and I wanted to get the shelter's AC fixed. I put the money in an envelope. I planned to give the five hundred to Paul the next morning. Even though it would be Sunday, Paul would be there checking on the animals before heading to the service at his church.

And it was also chance that I had trouble sleeping that night, and, before dawn, I got up and decided to check on the lot. Traffic was light and the sky was beginning to brighten when I turned onto Cleburne Road. I could tell by the lack of trash that Linda and the crew had recently cleaned Texas Pride. I parked in bay three, by the equipment room, and got out of my truck. As I unlocked the equipment room door and turned off the alarm, I noticed a burning smell. A quick check of the equipment showed that source wasn't any of my machines. I stepped out onto the lot and saw the faint glow of a fire coming from the front of the vet's, in the reception-office area. Why wasn't his alarm sounding? Then the howls and cries of the animals in the kennel startled me into action.

I kept a five-foot long crowbar, another tool someone left at the car wash, leaning against the wall beside the bill changer, and I grabbed the bar and ran across the parking lot to the vet's front door. Through the glass door I could clearly see flame starting to lick the wall beneath the window behind the computer station. The vet had a good lock on the door, but it couldn't stand up to the leverage of my long crowbar. Within seconds the door was open and I ran into the office, covering my mouth and nose with my t-shirt.

I immediately went to the back and opened the door to the fenced area beside the Texas Pride lot. The howls of the dogs and yowls of the cats in the kennel sparked me to hurry as I opened every cage and herded the animals outside into the fenced yard. I counted six dogs and three cats. There was nothing more I could do. I pulled the t-shirt across my face and rushed into the vet's one last time, wanting to be sure that I had not missed any cages in the small hospital, but the smoke had thickened. I couldn't breathe and I couldn't see, so I coughed my way back outside into the dawn and fresh air. The dogs ran nervously around the fence line as I fell to the ground, struggling to breathe. One of the freed cats, a black and white tabby, came over to me, as if to thank me for saving her, and then the next thing I knew a fireman was fitting an oxygen mask over my face as Paul held my head up.

"Fire inspector called it arson," Paul said. "It's a miracle you got everybody out."

It was two days after the fire. Although I had taken in some smoke, I had suffered no serious injury. We were having lunch at Carshon's, our neighbor across the alleyway and one of Paul's favorite restaurants. Paul took a big bite of his chopped liver sandwich. He had a side of potato salad with chips and a large pickle. I could see how he could put on a pound or two eating lunch at Carshon's four times a week. I looked at my humble grilled cheese.

"What did they find?"

"Gas can by the window," Paul said. "They broke the window, poured the gas down the wall, then lit it up."

"But what about your alarm? I didn't hear anything."

Paul took a sip of iced tea.

"They apparently cut the line to the outside siren, but the alarm still worked. The security company called me, the police, and the fire department. You must have nearly interrupted the arsonists."

"I don't know. I didn't see anybody. It's strange though. I've been having some gangster trouble because of this crazy fellow and a lost coin. They put a curse on my place, but the bad magic they hung on me shouldn't drift over to your shop."

Paul brushed a crumb off his mouth and leaned dangerously back in his chair.

"You've always got gangster trouble. No, more likely someone from the dark side of the vet world. People are nuts about their animals, and if we can't save them, sometimes things get crazy. Two weeks back, I couldn't help a spaniel, thirteen years old mind you. So the owner posts a Facebook calling me a dog killer. And back when I first bought the place, I got some pretty nasty graffiti. Could have been anyone I ticked off. Could have been from years back. Revenge is a dish best severed cold, like chopped liver."

He took a healthy bite of his sandwich.

"What are you going to do?

"Insurance will pay off, eventually. I'll take a little vacation and when I get a settlement I'll relocate. Somewhere a little less urban. Somewhere with affluent cat ladies and people with small dogs. You know, this was a nice neighborhood when your uncle bought the burned down dry cleaners and Dr. Jones, the first vet, opened the animal hospital. Hell, it was a nice neighborhood when I bought Jones out. But now?"

Paul waved his fork toward the window that looked out onto Cleburne Road. Litter from the train tracks blew across the street, and a prostitute and a homeless fellow were waiting out front at the bus stop.

"Not much here anymore except Carshon's and Texas Pride."

With Pam coming to visit I knew I had to count some coins and clean up the house. That night I counted and counted and counted until, finally, all but one bucket of quarters had been sacked into the thousand dollar bags I would deliver to the bank. I had put the chore off too long, but counting money was so boring that I had to smoke some of Gene's medical grade pot and drink a couple of beers to really get ready for the task. About half the time, I finished the joint and second beer just in time to remember to forget to count coins. Determined to finish counting all the coins I had collected, I dug into the last bucket of quarters. To my surprise, my first handful of quarters included not one, but two of the "magic" coins. They were the size of a quarter, but they were tinted gold, and each coin featured the naked woman with the "Heads I Win" and the "Tails You Lose" expression.

I fingered the coins, turning them both over and over and over in my palm.

"At last. Maybe that bastard will leave me alone."

I put the coins in the ashtray of the pickup truck so I could give them to Hammer the next time the gangsters appeared. But I didn't see them at the wash that day, and the temperatures remained hot and the sky remained cloudless.

Then they were there when I pulled up, parked in the drive, admiring my house. For a change, the gangsters were all wearing shirts, identical black pullovers.

I parked on the street and got out of the truck, my hand in my pocket, gripping the .32 auto.

"What are you doing here?"

"Came to see if you found our coin yet," Hammer said.

"How did you find my house?"

Hammer snorted, but he didn't smile.

"It wasn't hard. Lots of people watch you," he said, nodding toward the house. "Lots of people knows your place—Fort Knox of Fort Worth."

"Yeah, well, I have your coin."

Without turning my back on Hammer and his crew, I fetched one of the gold coins from the truck's ashtray.

"Is this what you're looking for?"

Hammer examined the coin carefully, inspecting both sides.

"That's it. What took you so long to find it?"

"I've been carrying it around hoping I'd run into you."

"You're a lucky man," he said. "You don't want to know. You don't mess with Hammer."

"Yeah, sure. Now leave me be."

Hammer and his buddies got into the Impala and sped off toward Berry Street. That was the last I ever saw of them; they never returned to the lot or to the house.

Then, almost magically, the equipment at the wash seemed to run smoother. The motors and pumps hummed efficiently, and the hoses stopped splinting. The temperature dropped into the seventies.

I stuffed five thousand dollars in fives into a large bag and took it to the animal shelter, an anonymous donation that would fix the AC and check the heat for the coming winter. And from that day on, I carried two things in my pocket: the .32 auto and the magic coin.

Chapter 9
Trip to Throckmorton

Finally, just after Halloween, summer seemed to end. The forecast for the weekend was cool and cloudy with a good chance of rain, and I figured that Texas Pride could run itself for one Saturday while I visited Pam in Throckmorton. I intended to stop in at the high school late Friday afternoon and then attend a football game–six man, the Throckmorton Greyhounds vs. the Knox City Greyhounds. The game was predicted to be a real dog fight.

I was not a big football fan. But football was king in the small towns of west Texas, even if there were only twelve players on the field. And Throckmorton had produced some notable players. Dallas Cowboy legend Bob Lilly played for Throckmorton until his family moved to Oregon his senior year, and fullback Pete Stout, who played for the Washington Redskins, was from Throckmoton.

Six-man ball had been around since the Depression, and I knew a little about the game from living in Grassland, which, like every other town in the region large enough to support a high school, had a six-man team. The field was shorter and narrower than in eleven-man ball, and the games tended to be high scoring. Scoring was a little different with six-man field goals worth four points, an extra point run worth one point, and the extra point kick worth two points.

All players were eligible receivers, and it took fifteen yards to get a first down. And, at least in Texas, there was a "mercy" rule stating that if a team had a forty-five point lead after the half, the game was over.

Knowing west Texas, I suspected that a lot of Throckmorton would be at the home game, and since Knox City was only fifty miles west (hundred mile round trip drives were considered short trips in that territory) there would be a good number of Knox City Greyhounds in the stands, too. I planned to attend the game and spend the night at the H&H Creek Inn in Seymour, thirty miles north on highway 283. Seymour, named after a local cowboy, Seymour Munday, was county seat of Baylor County and the intersection of five highways. You could get almost anywhere in Texas from Seymour.

Throckmorton didn't have a motel, and, for the sake of propriety, I couldn't stay at Pam's house. Throckmorton still required teachers to be role models as well as educators. It wasn't quite as bad as what Novalyne Price Ellis describes in *One Who Walked Alone*, her book about Robert Howard that was filmed under the title *The Whole Wide World*. Ellis taught in Cross Plains, not far from Throckmorton, and befriended (romanced?) Howard. She lived in a guest house with other women teachers and would have lost her job instantly if she had been caught drinking a beer or smoking a cigarette. Pam had it easy compared to Novalyne, but decorum still meant something in Throckmorton. If the weather improved, I would drive straight back to Fort Worth from Seymour Saturday morning so I could be at Texas Pride for the afternoon rush.

After checking the Texas Pride location one last time, I started out. I drove past the Squirt, Wipe and Go wash as I went down McCart Avenue. Squirt, Wipe and Go was an eight bay self serve, much like Texas Pride. Owen, a plump fifty-year old business professor at Tarrant County College owned the place. Squirt, Wipe and Go had a great location, right at the intersection of McCart and the I-20 bridge. Thirty or forty thousand cars a day drove by Squirt, Wipe and Go, and some of them were bound to stop. I recalled an article in the business section of the *Star-Telegram* that detailed plans to expand I-20 by two lanes and replace and widen the McCart street bridge. I wondered how that might affect Squirt, Wipe and Go. A construction project that would down the bridge at McCart would leave Owen's wash on a dead end street for a couple of years. I noticed that Owen's 1972 El Camino was on the lot, so I figured Owen was in the equipment room checking the machines.

I had met Owen a couple of times, once when he came by Texas Pride to borrow a validator for a coin changer and once when I went to Squirt, Wipe and Go to borrow a bladder tank for my pre soak system. Owen seemed like a reasonable fellow despite being an academic. Unlike their liberal arts counterparts, the business, nursing, and science professors still believe there is an objective reality. I had an eye on Owen's El Camino, which was one of the perks he allowed himself for owning a car-centric business. I stopped at the light at McCart and I-20, waiting to head west on the interstate. I had plenty of time to admire the bright red, fully restored car-truck. It would make a fine after-the-EMP vehicle because it lacked any computerized parts, and, in theory at least, would be fully functional post pulse.

I sped west on I-20, making up time because I wanted to be at the high school before the last period so I could visit the creative writing class Pam had told me about. There were eight students, a good crowd since there were fewer than two hundred students in the entire Throckmorton K-12 system.

The class was transforming the famous Thurber story "The Catbird Seat" into a one act play.

The afternoon was cool with clouds and a clear promise of rain, and the land, still summer-brown, was dry and broken. I took the back road up from Mineral Wells, skirting the north edge of Possum Kingdom Lake, following highway 16 to Graham. I turned west at Graham on highway 380 and felt the pressure of maintaining Texas Pride fade away with every mile that I drove. I was speeding through a special area of Texas sometimes called the Texas Midwest or the Big Country.

The Big Country was indeed big; it included the territory south of highway 380, east of the Caprock, north of I-10, and west of the Cross Timbers. Throckmorton County, on the northern edge of the Big Country, was especially empty: a thousand square miles and sixteen hundred people, about six hundred of them in the county seat of Throckmorton.

Throckmotorn had always been a remote area. The Spanish didn't make it through the region until the 1780s, in the 1850s it was the location of the Comanche Indian Reservation, and the Butterfield stage route snaked though the country in 1858. The Comanches were relocated to Oklahoma in 1861 just before the start of the Civil War. After the war, Fort Griffin protected buffalo hunters and settlers on what was then the edge of the frontier. The county was finally organized in 1879 and named for Dr. William Throckmorton, an early pioneer.

Visiting Thockmorton was like stepping back in time to the mid-twentieth century. Nearly everyone knew each other, nearly everyone attended football games on Friday night, and nearly everyone attended church on Sunday morning. Opening day of deer season was an unofficial holiday. Throckmorton was one of only twenty-two totally dry counties in Texas, so I had stashed a six pack of IPA in the cooler before leaving Ft. Worth.

I had traveled much of the region doing research for my article, "The Literary Big Country—Just How Big Is It?" I remembered my tenure review and Tim, the department chair, reacting when I told him that the piece would appear in the *Concho River Review*. ("*Concho River Review*," he had cackled. "You could hide fugitives in there.")

Place names on the map sparked my initial interest in the literary Big Country. Coke and Runells counties seemed especially literary. Some sixty or seventy miles southwest of Abilene, in Coke County, are the towns of Bronte and Tennyson, and in Runnells County there's a small community named Rowena. So within two neighboring counties were towns named after two of England's most famous writers, Charlotte Bronte (or could it be Emily Bronte?) and Alfred Lord Tennyson, and another named after a major character in Walter Scott's *Ivanhoe*.

I soon learned that the locals look at you like you're crazy if you ask them about the town of Bronte. They call the place *Bront*, and the name apparently was one of con- venience, chosen after the U. S. Postal Service rejected two early choices, *Oso*, which means *bear* in Spanish, and Bronco. About 1,000 people live in "Bront," and no one knows how many of them are familiar with the works of Charlotte or Emily Bronte. In 1882, an early settler from England named the neighboring town of Tennyson after the poet; at last count some thirty people live in Tennyson, just enough to preserve the post office. Rowena turns out not to have been named after the Scott character in *Ivanhoe* but after the wife of a railroad clerk. So there wasn't much to support my initial literary theory about the place names on the maps.

117

Rowena, however, does have some connection with popular literature as it is the birthplace of Bonnie Parker, of Bonnie and Clyde fame. Bonnie was a poet bank robber, author of "The Story of Bonnie and Clyde." It's a Robert Service style poem:

> Someday they'll go down together
> And they'll bury them side by side
> To few it'll be grief, to the law a relief
> But it's death for Bonnie and Clyde.

Other, more canonical, Big Country authors include Katherine Ann Porter, who is buried in the ghost town of Indian Creek. Porter, famous for *Ship of Fools* and *Pale Horse, Pale Rider,* set *Noon Wine* in central Texas, and one can see hints of her rural roots in a story like "The Jilting of Granny Weatherall." These days, Indian Creek no longer appears on the official road maps of the state, but the well-kept cemetery lies just off farm to market road 586, about three miles from what was the town of Indian Creek. A sign at the entrance to the cemetery warns visitors to beware of fire ants. Porter's headstone is not the largest in the small cemetery, but it has the most interesting inscription: "In My End Is My Beginning."

Not too many miles north of Indian Creek is the home of another Big Country writer who won world acclaim: Robert E. Howard. The pulp fiction author was born in Peaster, in Parker County, but lived in Cross Plains, which was an oil boom town in the 1920s when Howard began to publish in magazines such as *Weird Tales*. Howard is most famous for his Conan the Barbarian character, but he published more than 800 stories, poems, and novels before his death in 1936. Each June the town of Cross Plains hosts a Robert E. Howard festival, an event attended by fans from as far away as Asia and Europe.

On the eastern fringe of the Big Country is Putman, in Callahan County. Putman has two claims to fame; it is the home of the paper shell pecan and the birthplace of Texas playwright and author Larry L. King. When King was born in Putman in 1929, there may have been as many as 500 people living in the town. Today, the population is closer to twenty-five, and few visitors make it past the barbeque joint facing I-20 to the ghost town beyond the railroad tracks. King was nominated for a National Book Award for *Confessions of a White Racist*, but he is most famous for the play *The Best Little Whorehouse in Texas*.

But I didn't have to go through any of those literary towns on my way to Throckmorton. I just sped west on highway 380. I pulled into town, slowing as I passed the two small grocery stores and the abandoned two bay self service car wash, just in time for Pam's last class. The abandoned self serve illustrated the decline of Throckmorton; most any small town worth its salt had its own working two bay, and the more prosperous towns sometimes sported a four bay.

The high school itself was faced with an utilitarian brick that looked to be from the 1990s but it could have been older, and a two story gym anchored a long single story wing of classrooms. The middle school and elementary school were adjacent to the high school, so that all of Throckmorton ISD occupied a single block. The stadium was just out back, and it was smaller than I expected. The home-team benches could hold a couple of hundred people, and the visitors' benches half as many. The campus was neatly kept up, and from what I had seen coming into town, the courthouse, the churches (I spotted three) and the schools were clearly the best maintained buildings. There were lots of for sale signs, empty store fronts, and abandoned houses. The two grocery stores on Minter, an art studio that looked like a scrap metal junk yard, and the Allsup's were the only open businesses I saw.

I parked on College Street down from the school and walked past the stone monuments (almost like headstones) memorializing the Greyhounds' 2005 and 2011 state championship in six-man football and a 2003 state championship in class A Band. Each of the monuments was about four feet tall, made of granite with the top shaped into a map of Texas. The bottom half of each monument noted the members of the championship team.

A printed warning greeted me when I approached the high school. It was a poster-sized announcement taped to the glass window of the door:

ATTENTION
Please be aware that the staff of Throckmorton ISD
is armed and may use whatever force is
necessary to protect our students and staff.

Arming teachers, especially in remote areas, had become a popular policy as a result of a rash of school shootings that had plagued the nation in recent years. In the past, being a politically correct English professor, I would have objected to having armed teachers. Now, since I carried at least one gun nearly everywhere everyday, I had no problem with teachers carrying guns, especially in a place as remote as Throckmorton. There was only the sheriff and one deputy to patrol an area as large as Rhode Island, so calling 911 wouldn't do much good in a lot of situations.

I checked in with the secretary and she introduced me to Principal John Matthews, a bald-headed former coach. Principal John was dressed in slacks and a button-down white shirt, no tie, and plain black cowboy boots. I suspected that he kept a Glock locked in an easily accessible desk drawer. Pam had told John that I planned to visit, so we exchanged pleasantries and a student escorted me to Pam's classroom.

I was amazed at how small the school was: just a wing of classrooms and a couple of rows of lockers. There were only about sixty students in the high school, and Pam worked with three other teachers. The math teacher also directed the band, the science teacher also taught Spanish, the coach also taught history (of course), and Pam covered English and humanities. Most schools as small as the Throckmorton system would have been consolidated, but as the county seat of a vast county, Throckmorton had a lot of staying power.

Pam smiled when I entered the room. I could feel her eyes dancing across my body.

"Students," she said to her class. "I want to introduce you to my good friend and former professor, Dr. Leonard Edwards."

The eight students smiled. I recognized Andy Wilson, the student who had won the cowboy poetry contest at the Red Steagall festival. We nodded at each other as Pam introduced me to the other students, a clean cut mix of polite boys and girls. Throckmorton was only a few hours from the urban mess of Dallas-Fort Worth, but it seemed like another planet, almost as if I had twilight-zoned back into the 1950s when teachers were respected members of the community instead of clowns.

Pam and the students had a lively discussion of the technical aspects of transforming Thurber's 1942 short story into a one-act play. "Catbird Seat" was a good subject for such a project due to the story's snappy dialogue and limited, interior settings.

Andy was going to play the part of Erwin Martin, the boring and predictable head of the filing department at F&S,

the corporation run by Mr. Fitweiler, the F of F&S. Fitweiler has fallen under the seductive influence of Ulgine Barrows, a woman whose ambitions are to transform F&S into something of her liking and whose conversations are characterized by such expressions as "Don't tear up the pea patch," and "Are you sitting in the catbird seat?" An attractive junior named Alice Anne would play Barrows. Making Alice Anne look twenty-years older for the capstone performance would be a challenge.

"Are you lifting the ox cart out of the ditch?" Alice Anne asked Andy, practicing the opening line in the play.

The class had done a fine job, with a little assistance from Pam I was sure, in rearranging the action in the story in order to limit the setting of the play to two rooms—the F&S office and Barrows' apartment. That limited setting would serve the class well when the students presented the play as part of their theater instruction. The necessary background material would be conveyed via dialogue. I was impressed with the effort the students put into the project. Pam told me that the class would present the play at a school assembly right before the holidays.

After class, Pam and I shared stale coffee with her colleagues in the room they called teachers' lounge. The other teachers were all long time locals. It was the sort of place where you either fit in or you didn't. Pam seemed to have made the cut, which didn't surprise me since she was a cowgirl from a small town herself and anyone with any sense would see she was a good person and a great teacher.

"So, have you two known each other long," Pam's principal, John, asked.

"I was one of her professors at South East Panhandle State, Grasslands, a few years back. That was before I went into business in Fort Worth."

"What do you do?

"I own a car wash. You know. The coin op kind where you start the bay up and wash the car yourself."

"Big change from professoring. Bet it's a cash cow."

"That's what everybody tells me."

"Well, we're glad Pam came to teach with us. I had to promise to look into the possibility of establishing a rodeo club for her to coach. It's still an 'idea' at this stage. Just so few students."

"But they seem to be good ones."

Big Bald John laughed and slapped me on the back. You can't take the coach out the coach, no matter what.

We had a bit of time to kill before the game, so Pam drove us out of town about ten miles to visit Throckmorton's most famous work of art: a twenty-two foot tall rusting steel longhorn bull with its nose to the air, sniffing for cows. Joe Barrington, a local artist, constructed the work, called *Bridle Bit Bull* in 2011; the bull had become a famous roadside attraction, more popular even than the giant armadillo in nearby Buffalo Gap. We spotted the longhorn several miles before we reached him on the side of highway 380. The bull was enormous but was dwarfed by the vast open landscape behind it.

We pulled off the road and parked directly in front of the statue. There was nothing between us and the huge work of art other than a barbed wire fence that Pam quickly jumped. The wind had picked up and I buttoned my jacket. Pam, who had visited the work often, stood beneath the giant longhorn.

"It's my favorite place near Throckmorton," Pam said. "Art that 'fits.'"

The bull was the world's largest steel longhorn. He was a red rust monster with great horns and with his snout high in the air. His face had been nicked by bullets more than a few times, but those dings just gave the figure more character as he lifted his nose to the ever present wind, forever sniffing for cows in heat.

"I know the artist, too," Pam continued. "He also had the world's largest buffalo skull on display in Abilene."

"So world's largest is his forté. How did you meet him?"

"He's got a studio in Throckmorton. I see him once in a while Clint's or the Allsup's."

"I think I drove past his studio when I came into town. Looks like a scrap metal dump."

"That's his place," Pam said. "All that metal waiting to become art."

We circled the statue a time or two and headed back to town for the game.

It was a good night for football, in the sixties with a slight north wind. As was so often the case, the promise of rain had proved false. The clouds had thinned after sunset, making me think that I might have a pretty good Saturday at Texas Pride.

Pam and I were quite the show at the game; she was the only unmarried teacher in the school system and the youngest, too, from what I could see. Everyone seemed to be curious about this out-of-town fellow Pam had brought to the game. It was almost as if the entire town was sizing me up, trying to determine my odds of marrying Pam and moving into their world. I met more of Pam's students, and plenty of parents.

The evening was like a night in a Norman Rockwell painting: seemingly endless introductions to students and parents and standing for the pledge before the game. The only thing missing was a prayer; even Throckmorton had been touched by the Supreme Court rulings. As old fashioned as it was (and I was certain there were tensions I could not see) there was a true sense of community, especially compared to the chaos that reigned on the streets of Ft. Worth-Dallas just a few hours to the east.

There were lots of Knox City fans in the stands, and I found it a little confusing to have two opposing teams both cheering for the "Greyhounds." The announcers settled the confusion by calling the plays by town name rather than mascot. Sometime they combined both: "And the Throckmorton Greyhounds take the lead over Knox City, here, in Throckmoton. Early in the first quarter it's the Throckmorton Greyhounds with eight points after that two point extra kick and the Knox City Greyhounds yet to score."

Principal John was in line for a hot dog when Pam and I walked up to the concession stand. I had decided on a standard dog, no onions, and a cup of coffee. Pam wanted a hamburger and a coke. Other than tobacco, which wasn't allowed on school grounds, caffeine was the strongest legal drug in town.

"So what did you think of Pam's creative writing class?" John asked me.

"Thought it was great. I like the idea of producing the play after it's written. Good combination of literature and theater."

"Yes," he said, moving a bit closer to the concession stand, following the line. "In a district this small we have to be jacks of all trades. We're lucky to have Pam with us."

Pam blushed a bit.

"She was my best student at SEPSU. The only one to get a Master's."

"I wasn't that great," Pam said with a smile. "But I was the teacher's pet."

Big Bald John raised an eyebrow and stepped up to the stand for his hot dog with Pam and me close behind.

The second half didn't go well for the Knox City dogs. And by the early forth quarter, with Throckmorton having a thirty-five point lead, I was ready to head to Seymour and call it a long day. Pam and I left the stadium and walked to my truck, which was still parked out front of the high school.

"Wish you could stay the night," Pam said, "but I've already got the gossip mill running with that 'teacher's pet' comment."

"It's okay. You've got a fine thing going here. Don't let me mess it up."

"It's a good enough job and Throckmorton's an okay town, if you don't mind the isolation. The people have been really welcoming."

"Maybe we should think more about getting married," I said, too abruptly, I realized as I spoke. "Then I could move in with you here."

Pam looked at me in the dim light as we stood by my truck. Her eyes were two deep pools of blue.

"I know we talked about it, Leonard, and you know I love you. But you've never been married. It's more complicated than you think. 'Marriage is not a safe anchorage but a voyage on uncharted seas.'"

"Well, sure. But 'No power on earth can e'er dive the knot that sacred love hath tied.'"

Pam laughed. This sort of game had become familiar to us in the long Panhandle winter nights. Pam usually won because, as much as I hated to admit it, her memory was better than mine.

"You had a bad experience the first time," I said. "But you know I love you. We could make it work. I know we could."

Pam shook her head doubtfully.

"Let's give it some time. There's lots to think about. Where to live. Kids? Money. I'm not twenty any more and I don't want to mess up again."

We stood there a few moments, looking at the stars in the clearing sky.

"Weather is improving. I'll have good business tomorrow."

"You'll want to get back early."

"This is a ridiculous situation. I'm saddled with a business hours away from your world."

"No, go on. Maybe we can met in Graham in a couple of weeks."

"What about the holidays?"

"I'm going to Perryton to see my folks but I'm coming to Fort Worth right before Thanksgiving. There's an exhibit coming to the Cowgirl Museum that I want to catch. You go on now. Drive careful."

She kissed me good night, and I drove off, heading north on 283 through the emptiness to my room in Seymour, thirty miles away. Just before the Baylor County line I pulled over at a wide spot and took a long piss under the windy, clearing sky. I popped an IPA and stared at the stars as they began to appear above the Big Country.

Chapter 10
Trouble at the Museum

There are a lot of things that Fort Worth doesn't have, oceans and mountains, for instance, but Fort Worth does have some fine museums. Five of the best of these museums are located close together in what the natives call the "cultural district." I had been to all of the big five, and I drove through the area frequently because all the gun shows were held at the Will Rodgers Memorial Center, which is where the museum goers usually park. The Kimbell Art Museum has a eclectic collection of masters housed in a distinctive Louis I. Kahn "light is the theme" building. The nearby Amon Carter Museum of American Art hosts an outstanding collection anchored by Remingtons and Russells, and the Modern Art Museum of Fort Worth, housed in five flat-roofed, glass-walled pavilions designed by Japanese architect Tadao Ando, features post World War II art in any medium. Also in the Cultural District is the Fort Worth Museum of Science and History, favorite of families with young children. Pam liked all the museums, but being a cowgirl, she liked the Cow Girl Museum and Hall of Fame best of all. In fact, Pam's current excuse for visiting was an exhibit at the Cow Girl: the wagon and camping equipment Georgia O'Keeffe used when she painted in the New Mexico outback.

Pam discovered a lot of reasons to visit Fort Worth since we found each other at Texas Pride. I was, of course, the one main reason, but food and culture placed high on the list. The culture of Throckmorton was limited: church, school, football, deer season. As for food, Throckmorton had two small but adequate grocery stores and a twenty-four hour Allsup's that specialized in fried everything. If you wanted vegetables at the Allsup's, there were bean burrito *chimichangas* and rumors that someday there might be pre-packaged salads. For Pam it was a sixty-mile round trip drive to the supermarket in Seymour or in Haskell. Pam usually drove to Haskell, which was a bit farther, since there were actual liquor stores where she could buy wine. Seymour, in Baylor County, only allowed beer sales, and of course, Throckmorton was completely dry. So food was a big part of a visit to Fort Worth. Pam kept an ice chest in the trunk of the Crown Victoria, and she usually stopped at Central Market and stocked up on the way back to Throckmorton from Fort Worth.

She planned to drive in after class on the Friday before Thanksgiving. We would have late dinner Friday night and visit the Cow Girl on Saturday. Sunday Pam would drive back to Throckmorton for a short pre-holiday school week before heading up to Perryton to spend Thanksgiving with her folks. She was putting a lot of miles on the Crown Vic, and I made a mental note to check the vehicle when Pam arrived.

"I've come to a decision," Pam said, pausing over her chopsticks for a moment.

We were at the Szechuan in City View, one of Pam's favorite Chinese restaurants. I liked the Szechuan because the food was good and the location was convenient. I figured

Saturday night would be either Mexican (probably Benito's on Magnolia) or Italian (probably Prima's Pasta off Hulen).

"Oh, yeah?"

"About us," Pam said, putting down her sticks and looking me in the eyes.

"Don't hold back."

After my clumsy attempt of proposing had been rebuffed when I visited Throckmorton, I was a little unsure about the situation. But her look was lovingly serious.

"I've done a lot of thinking since your visit. It's really lonely in Throckmorton, surrounded by all the married couples with families. You know I love you, and I know you love me. I blew it on the first run, but I'm older now, a lot more mature, and I'm willing to try again. We can get married, if you want, and if we agree on a few principles."

This was progress, for sure.

"I'll have to buy a ring," I said. "I haven't found any good ones in the vacs lately."

Pam laughed.

"You don't have to hurry. Principle number one is to be patient. It might be a long engagement, like maybe until the end of the school year next spring."

"Okay."

"Principle number two is that we probably will want a kid or two in the first five years. I'm not getting any younger."

"Okay."

"Principle number three is that I'll have to have a place where I can keep my horse, Tex, and eventually some other horses. Somewhere near Throckmorton because I don't plan to leave my job."

"Okay."

"Principle number four is you have to work, bring in some money. I don't want to support a house husband in Throckmorton, or anywhere else for that matter."

The principles were mounting up.

"Okay. It'll take a while to figure out the logistics of running Texas Pride while you're in Throckmorton. But I'm willing if you are."

Pam lifted her glass of wine.

"To us."

I tapped her glass with my beer.

"To us," I said.

We took the Crown Victoria to Will Rodgers because I wanted to test drive the car and swing through the gun show before we visited the Cow Girl. I was looking for some hard to find ammo for one of Jake's old revolvers, a .38 Colt Police Positive that I guessed was from the 1920s. How and why Uncle Jake had this pistol would always be a mystery, but I had found it clean and holstered in the back shelf of his gun cabinet. It was one of those times when I wished my dad or Jake were still alive so they could provide me some history about the pistol. I wondered if it had belonged to my grandfather on my dad's side; he had owned a gas station in south Texas for many years. The revolver took a short Colt .38 cartridge, not the more common .38 special, and the Colt .38 rounds were becoming more and more expensive and more and more difficult to locate. Hopefully, one of the ammo dealers at the show would have a box or two in stock.

Pam and I breezed though the check in at the gun show; I wasn't carrying so we didn't have to stop and have a gun examined by a police officer who would make certain the weapon was unloaded. This show was like most others, well attended because Texans love their guns. The exhibit hall was

divided into corridors lined on both sides by tables. Everything was clean, well lit, and well organized, but since the sale
of beer at the gun shows had been prohibited, a lot of the old
time fun was missing. Still, there was just about anything this
side of full auto that a gunner might want. Each table
specialized in certain types of weapons: semi-auto rifles,
semi-auto pistols, revolvers, shotguns, antiques. An older
man carried a slung lever-action rifle on his shoulder, a for
sale sign ($600) protruding from the barrel. In Texas
individuals could still buy and sell guns from each other
without background checks. All the dealers at the tables were
licenced, and they were able to run sales though the FBI
instantly. There was also gear and food for hunters,
survialists, and outdoors lovers; Pam bought a pouch of
buffalo jerky.

I spotted a table selling ammo, but I didn't see any
Colt. .38.

"What you looking for, mister?"

The table's manager was a stocky fellow in his forties
with a rough stubble of beard.

"I need some ammo for a Colt. 38 Police Positive. It
takes a .38 Colt short."

"Let's see what I can find."

He went to the back of the booth and sorted though a
crate of ammo. He returned with two boxes of Remington
Performance Wheel Gun in .38 short Colt. Each box
contained fifty rounds.

"Got these two, that's all. Forty bucks a box."

"Okay. It's getting expensive, and hard to find."

"Oh you'll be alright so long as Remington keeps these
in production. You could also use Smith and Wesson .38, not
the .38 special. If you can't find any at a show, try on-line. I'd

save the brass, though, in case you need to reload your own some day."

I counted out eighty dollars in fives and placed them on the table while he bagged up my ammo.

We left the jerky and the ammo in the Crown Vic and walked across the parking lot to the Cow Girl. Families with kids were leaving the Natural Science Museum and looking for their cars as the gun show customers packed their weapons and ammo into their trucks.

The Cow Girl Museum had a long history. It began in 1975 in Hereford, Texas, where the collection consisted mostly of western art housed in the basement of the Deaf Smith County library. In the 1980s, the expanded collection was stored in a private home. Finally, the museum's board of directors launched a plan to find a new location for the collection, somewhere easily accessible to the public. The choice was the museum district in Fort Worth. According to the museum's information, the building, designed by David Schwarz and opened in 2002, reflects the cowgirl way of life in bas-relief and "wild rose finials." But the structure always reminded me of a small, three story castle, like something you would see in the Scottish highlands, except with cowgirls on horses in the bas-reliefs. There are two hundred forty or so members of the Cow Girl Hall of Fame, reflecting a wide range of western life; among the more well know are Annie Oakley, Dale Evans, Reba McEntire, Sandra Day O'Connor, and, of course, Georgia O'Keeffe.

Pam and I paid our admission fee and entered the museum. The O'Keeffe exhibit took up a prominent place on the first floor. The exhibit was called "Georgia O'Keeffe and the Far Away: Nature and Image." The display was a detailed recreation of one of O'Keeffe's campsites in New Mexico, where she frequently camped to find inspiration for her paintings. In fact, the campsite was framed by nine of O'Keeffe's paintings and a couple of dozen photographs and some sketches.

Any lover of the outdoors immediately saw that things had changed, but not that much, since O'Keeffe's camping days. There was the familiar camp table, only O'Keeffe's was made of wood, a camp chair, cook kit, and canvas tent. On the wooden camp table O'Keeffe's notebook lay open.

"Makes me want to go to New Mexico," Pam said.

"We should go out to Ghost Ranch some time."

We made our way up to the second floor, taking in information about the Hall of Fame members. A poster announced a coming exhibit called "Hitting the Mark," about cowgirls in the wild west shows.

"I've got to come back for that one," Pam said. "Those shows were the start of women's rodeos, you know."

Then came a thundering crash from the first floor and someone shouted "Stop! Stop!" Then another crash and a moan. We ran down the stairs and saw the overturned Georgia O'Keeffe camp table and a couple of men rolling on the floor in front of the door to the museum. One of the men was a security guard, and the other a slightly built man wearing a black cowboy hat and clutching a notebook in his right hand. The security guard finally penned the man face down to the ground then zapped him with a taser, making the man lose his hat and the notebook. Within seconds, another guard ran up and placed cuffs on the offender.

Pam and I were only a few yards away when the guards turned the man face up.

It was a cowboy poet.

The incident made the metro section of the next day's
Star-Telegram.

English Professor Attempts Theft at Cowgirl Museum

Police report that a fifty-three year old man was arrested
Saturday afternoon at the Cow Girl Museum and Hall of Fame. The
man was identified as Timothy Collard of Grassland, Texas. He was
charged with felony theft and resisting arrest. Witnesses report that
Collard, an English Professor and Chair of the English Department
at South East Panhandle State University in Grassland, attempted
to steal a journal from the Georgia O'Keeffe camping exhibit on
display at the Cow Girl Museum. Collard allegedly took the journal
from its place on a camp table in the display and attempted to exit
the museum with the journal in his hand. After a short altercation
with security guards, Collard was arrested and taken by Fort Worth
Police officers to the Mansfield detention center where he is being
held pending bond. Witnesses say that Collard admitted to stealing
the journal on "impulse" because it was rumored to contain a rare
"cowgirl" poem written by O'Keeffe on the occasion of her
watercolor, *Train Coming in Canyon*. Collard is a well known
cowboy poet; he judged the cowboy poetry contest at last year's
Red Steagall Cowboy Gathering in the Stockyards, and his most
recent book, *When Cows Cry*, has won numerous awards. The
President of South East Panhandle State University did not respond
to emails or phone calls concerning Dr. Collard's arrest.

Chapter 11
Squirt, Wipe and Gone

Thanksgiving was just like every other day at Texas Pride, a work day, except that after the fire, Paul wasn't around the to walk the dogs at the vet's. It was just me and the regular management of the lot. The weather was fine, cool and clear, and when the men folk got tired of hanging around their families and when the football games didn't turn out to be too exciting, the car wash offered a convenient escape. Business was good, and I couldn't complain about working. Pam was in Perryton with her family, and I didn't have anything better to do. In fact, she sent me a text:

"I made it to Perryton just before dark Wednesday. I told mom and dad about the engagement, and they are excited and are looking forward to meeting you. Anyway, don't work too hard. Love you!"

Pam and I were the rare people who used correct spelling and punctuation in our texts. Maybe that's why we didn't text much.

Throckmorton had let school out at noon on the Wednesday before Thanksgiving. It was an easy four and a half hour drive from Throckmorton to Perryton, but I always worried about Pam when she made the trip. I decided to keep an eye out for a newer, more reliable car. The old Crown Victoria was a settlement from her divorce. Her husband had owned an used car lot in Amarillo, but he had gone bankrupt. That explained why Pam was insistent that we both work, make some money, follow principle number four. It would be a challenge, though, to manage Texas Pride while Pam taught in the boondocks, but I would find a way.

I was on a ladder, changing a motor on a vac, when Owen drove his El Camino onto the lot. The El Camino attracted attention everywhere, and a couple of customers pointed at the odd car-pickup truck combination.

"What's up, Leo?" Owen said, walking over and standing by the vac I was repairing.

"Just changing out a vac motor, you know. How are you?"

"I'm good. Only a couple more weeks to go in the semester."

I didn't know Owen very well, but l had met him a couple of times when we loaned each other spare parts for the machines. When he was washing cars, he always wore black boots, black pants, and a bright, red long-sleeved shirt. The shirt was emblazoned with the Squirt, Wipe and Go logo right above the pocket, a trigger wand spraying water. Wearing that work shirt, Owen was a blaze of red when he drove around in the red El Camino.

"Give me a minute and I'll be finished with this."

I rewired the motor.

"Hand me that vac cover, please."

Owen lifted the stainless steel cover up to me. I bolted the cover over the top of the vac and came down the ladder.

"Seems like these motors are not holding up like they should," I said, tossing the bad one in the trash. "What brings you down this way?"

"Don't know if you follow the business section in the *Star-Telegram*, but maybe you've heard about the expansion of I-20 just off my lot at Squirt, Wipe and Go."

"Yeah, I remember that. Are they going to actually start the project."

"Looks like it's a sure thing. I was worried it might cost me some business but that turns out to be a moot point."

"What do you mean?"

"Eminent domain. I just had a long meeting with the state highway and transportation people. When they blow the bridge across McCart, they plan to take out my car wash and an entire line of houses on the north side of I-20 all the way to Westcreek. In six months from now Squirt, Wipe and Go will be history."

This was an unexpected event.

"What are you going to do?"

"I came to make you a deal."

The second week in December a norther blew through and I was able to escape from Texas Pride for a night. Pam and I were under the blankets in our room at the Best Western Plus in Graham. We had feasted on Chinese take out from the Golden China restaurant. It was good food, maybe not as good as the Szechuan, but certainly better than anything at the Allsup's in Throckmorton. Over the last few months we had gotten to know most of the motels in Graham, and the Best Western was a favorite. Graham was a forty-five minute straight-shot drive east on 380 from Throckmorton, and about an hour an a half drive west from Fort Worth. When the weather looked rainy or cold, Pam and I could meet for a night in Graham and she would still be able to make it to class the next day without trouble. I was even considering renting a house in Graham after the wedding.

"You should take Owen up on his offer," Pam said. "Then you can move to Throckmorton and we can be together all the time."

"But what could I do in Throckmorton? What about principle number four?"

"Cost of living is cheap. You could live on interest and investment income after the sale, and we can get you on my health insurance after we are married."

Pam was very practical for an English major. She was a Realist, a close academic relation to a Naturalist like me.

"Four hundred thousand isn't that much," I said.

I failed to mention the other two hundred fifty thousand in cash that Jake had left me or the fifty thousand in quarters that I had stashed. It was all in fives and coins and I hadn't figured out how to use it. Two hundred fifty thousand in fives would buy a lot of groceries, gas, and beer in Seymour or Haskel, not to mention fried food at the Allsup's.

"Maybe you could teach again. The junior college in Cisco is only an hour's drive from Throckmorton."

An hour each way on those empty highways was nothing. I thought of all the poor commuters in the metromess that is DFW who sat in traffic jams for hours each week.

"That's an idea. And there's that abandoned two bay in Throckmorton. I could rebuild that place for next to nothing, but I'm not sure I would ever make any money out of it. I could call it Greyhound Pride Car Wash."

"That would certainly endear you to the community," Pam said. "Have to join a church, too. I've visited them all several times. I won't tell you my favorite until you've seen them yourself."

We were both unchurched believers, like a lot of people our age.

"Do you really think we can be happy in Throckmorton? We'll always be in the small town public eye."

"We can be happy anywhere."

She snuggled up closer to me, warm as fire on a cold night.

What was it about the chopped liver at Carshon's? Owen wolfed down his sandwich.

"So good," he said.

Classes were out, finals over, and he had just turned in his grades for the semester, which explained why Owen was wearing slacks and a dress shirt instead of his red and black Squirt, Wipe and Go outfit. Pam still had another week of school in Throckmorton, and she planned to spend Christmas with her folks in Perryton and then visit me in Fort Worth before classes began just after New Year's. Pam's parents had wanted me to come with her, but I explained that Texas Pride couldn't run itself. Besides, if things worked out as I hoped, there would be plenty of time for me to meet the family before the wedding, which was still planned for some unknown date in the distant summer.

I took a bite of my chicken salad.

"Owen, I know I told you that I used to teach English at South East Panhandle State, up in Grassland."

"Yeah, sure."

"Well, what I wonder is how you manage to walk in two worlds at the same time without going crazy. I mean, we both know what the street life of a self service coin op car wash is like. And then you seamlessly become a business professor dealing with students, faculty, and administrators instead of bums, prostitutes, and thieves."

"You know, Tarrant County College isn't exactly Harvard. And the work schedule for business professors isn't exactly eight to five. But I keep both worlds in separate compartments. The only thread connecting the two is the El Camino which takes me to and from each world."

Owen took sip of his iced tea.

"I will admit that the robbery last year did shake me up a bit," he said.

The story of Owen's mugging was well known. Three masked assailants relieved him of all his bill changer money, holding him at Glock point in the equipment room and emptying the machines of bills and coins.

"Do you carry a weapon."

"No. I'd be more likely to shoot myself than a bad guy."

"I've thought over your offer," I said. "We both know that four hundred is a reasonable price. Fair to us both. So I won't bother haggling over that with you. But I do have two requests."

"Yeah. What's that?"

"First is that you keep on my crew if I sell to you. You know Gary since he's already working for you at Squirt, Wipe and Go. Besides him there's just Linda and Doyle, the clean up crew, and Lloyd, who checks the machines each day. He doesn't charge much and he's likely to quit at any time, but he lives near Texas Pride and it's nice to have a spare set of eyes in the neighborhood."

"Sure," Owen said. "I'll need the help anyway. What else?"

"If the highway department is going to tear down Squirt, Wipe and Go, I figure you'll be salvaging your equipment for spares or for sale. I want you to throw in the motors and pumps and equipment for two complete self serve bays."

Owen thought it over for a moment.

"Okay. But why do you want that?"

"Let me tell you about this old two bay I've located in Throckmorton."

Pam and I celebrated New Year's Eve by picking up a six pack of IPA and a bottle of wine at the liquor store, then settling down for a home cooked meal back at the house. I made black eyed peas and gumbo z'herbes, seven lucky greens. Gumbo z'herbes was a traditional dish my mother had learned to cook when she taught for a brief spell in Louisiana before moving to Fort Worth where she met my father, at church, of course. Mom was a little bit superstitious, and she made the seven lucky greens each New Year's to guarantee good luck. She made gumbo z'herbes the New Year's Day the year of the trip to Thailand. But Mom and Dad's luck ran out when they went below deck for lunch on the ferry from Samui to Phangan.

I was using the day's *Star-Telegram* as a sheet to dry the freshly washed greens when I noticed the story updating Tim Collard's arrest at the Cow Girl.

Professor Makes Plea Deal in Museum Theft

English Professor Timothy Collard of Grasslands, Texas, has accepted a plea arrangement with the Tarrant County district attorney. Collard, who was Chair of the English Department at South East Panhandle State University, pled guilty to one count of felony theft. Charges of resisting arrest were dropped as part of the agreement which places Collard on probation for ten years. Collard has also agreed to pay a twenty thousand dollar fine.

Collard was arrested last fall when he attempted to steal a journal from the Georgia O'Keeffe exhibit at the Cow Girl Hall of Fame and Museum. Collard stated that he took the journal from the exhibit on "impulse" because he had heard a rumor that O'Keeffe had written a cowgirl poem in the journal and he wanted to add it to his extensive collection of rare cowboy poetry. Collard is a well known cowboy poet himself. He served as judge for the cowboy poetry contest at last year's Red Steagall Cowboy Gathering in the Stock Yards. His most recent book, *When Cows Cry*, has received critical acclaim for "putting the cow back in cowboy poetry." It is unclear at this time if Professor Collard will continue to teach at South East Panhandle State University, but he has resigned as Chair of the English Department.

"Looks like Tim is in for a tough time," Pam said. "Serves him right."

"I wonder if SEPSU will let him keep his job. Not likely since he pled guilty to a felony."

"Do you think there really was a rare poem in that journal."

"I would guess not or we would have read about it by now. But there could be a job opening in the department soon."

I wouldn't be applying even if a job at Grassland opened up. I was committed to Pam and Throckmorton and rebuilding the two bay that had served as a storage shed since it was closed in the early 1980s. I had Pam work on permits and utilities since she was living in Throckmorton and I still had Texas Pride to maintain. When the weather clouded up, I took to spending a couple days at a time clearing the exterior and the lot at the two bay. The equipment room was full of junk and I knew I would need help hauling away all the debris. I spent the nights in Seymour, keeping up a good front for the locals since Pam and I weren't married yet.

144

True to his word, Owen delivered two motors, two pumps, two coin receivers and timers, two of just about everything I would need to reconstruct the car wash in Throckmorton. In late March, Owen and I stood across McCart from his lot and watched the highway department bulldoze the red brick shell of his car wash. Squirt, Wipe and Go was now Squirt, Wipe and Gone.

Chapter 12
Waiting for Marriage (and the EMP)

I always tell my students in the Intro to Fiction class that fiction is nothing like life. Fiction, and literature in general, is an attempt to make sense of the chaos that is our lives, to put an envelope of meaning around events. In a novel or short story, there is usually an effort to give events a shape, to wrap up the narrative in some clever way. Readers like the tight, ironic endings that characterize stories by O'Henry or Maupassant because they so clearly demonstrate the themes of the tales and signal a clear summing up.

Unlike fiction, life is messy, shaped by chance or what some call fate, and usually devoid of neat wrap ups other than death. That's why I'm a literary Naturalist; Naturalism is the type of fiction that I think most clearly reflects the actual world. Chance, heredity, biological needs, and the indifference of nature are the true shapers of our lives. It was chance and the indifference of nature that led to my parents' drowning in a ferry accident in Thailand. I might have become a professor at SEPSU or some other school where I could have spent my days in bland academic buildings attending stuffy faculty meetings; instead chance intervened when my uncle Jake died and left me the Texas Pride Car Wash. And if the highway department hadn't decided to expand I-20, blow up the McCart Street bridge, and bulldoze Owen's Squirt, Wipe and Go wash, I wouldn't have been able to sell the Texas Pride location and move to Throckmorton. The highway department was a sort of deus ex machina in my Texas Pride story, and the machina was a bulldozer.

I wished Owen luck with Texas Pride as I left the lawyer's office in downtown Fort Worth with a check for $400,000 in my wallet. I knew that Owen would take good care of the car wash; he was a pro. And in addition to the check, I had the house in Westcliff and the quarter million in fives from Jake's closet and about fifty thousand in quarters that I had held back in the months since Owen proposed the sale. I would be able to launder the currency and coin after I opened up the two bay. Eventually, I would sell the house in Westcliff and use the proceeds as a down payment on a small farm off of highway 380, some ten miles west of Throckmorton.

Pam had announced our engagement to her colleagues, and they seemed genuinely pleased. After they passed the test of time, outsiders were welcome in a small town with a declining population. Each Sunday, we visited a different church. There were five of them: the First United Methodist, the First Baptist, a Church of Christ, a New Life Assembly of God, and the Christian Center of Throckmorton. We had pretty much settled on the Methodists since I had been reared a Methodist and Pam's family was Presbyterian. If you were a teacher in Throckmorton, it didn't matter which church you attended, but you better join one and show up for services on a good number of Sundays.

The wedding would be in Perryton on June 30, and Pam had made reservations for our honeymoon at the Calgary Stampede in Alberta, Canada.

"It's the world's largest rodeo," Pam said. "Some of the world's best barrel racers will be there. I booked a whole week at the Hotel Arts. It's downtown and only a ten minute walk to Stampede Park."

While waiting for the magic date to arrive, we were determined to keep up appearances, so I continued to avoid spending any nights with Pam in Throckmotorn. Instead, I took a room by the week at the H&H Inn in Seymour and made the thirty minute commute each morning to Throckmorton where I would work on the two bay until meeting Pam after school. I could buy beer in Seymour, and that meant a lot because I was usually ready for a few brews after working all day at the two bay. Reopening a self serve that had been shut down for decades turned out to be a serious job. The oversized equipment room was full of abandoned car parts and other trash, so I hired the Throckmorton football team to help me clear the lot and haul the junk to the dump. The pits were full of sand and dirt and had to be pumped by a company from Abilene. It took a few weeks to have the plumbing and electrical up and working, and then I was able to begin installing equipment and lines.

Owen had been more than generous with the equipment from Squirt, Wipe and Go.

"I've got more spare parts than I'll ever need," he explained.

So in addition to the two motors, pumps, and safes I had asked for, I got high and low pressure lines, an air compressor for the tire clean and pre soak systems, and two stainless steel vacuums. Owen also tossed in a couple of soap holding tanks, a bunch of spare parts and a change machine. The water heater was the only piece of new equipment I had to buy. It was quite the haul, and I stored the equipment in the garage at Pam's house. In early June, just as the real heat begin to set in, I bought the mini farm about ten miles west of town off highway 380.

One day at the high school I had mentioned that I was looking for a place out of town where we could eventually keep Pam's horse, a small place, something the locals would call a hobby ranch. Land, I had discovered, was surprisingly expensive, and I was getting discouraged. A few days later I got a call from Jim Wilson. I had met Jim and his wife Lynda at the Red Steagall Cowboy Gathering. Their son, Andy, was a student in Pam's class. He had won the cowboy poetry contest and had read his poem at the Steagall event. Jim and Lynda had a ranch about ten miles west of Throckmorton. Their place was about a hundred thousand acres, some of it guarded by the *Bridle Bit Bull* that watched over highway 380 west of town.

"Andy told me you were looking for a place to keep a horse. I have something that might interest you," Jim told me.

"Okay, but Andy doesn't know how little money I have."

"Meet me at the big bull," he said, meaning the *Bridle Bit* on 380. "Three tomorrow afternoon."

It was a blazing hot afternoon when Jim pulled up to the giant bull in his nearly new Ford F-150 dual cab pickup. The truck was white, a popular color in hot country since it reflected so much sunlight and heat. Jim hadn't changed much since the cowboy gathering; he was still wearing boots, jeans, and a white shirt and white cowboy hat. He shook my hand energetically, as if he were greeting a long lost friend. People are like that in West Texas, friendly until you give them a reason not to be.

"Congratulations," he said. "Andy told me that you and Pam were going to tie the knot."

"Yes. Looks like it's going to happen. Last of June."

"Everybody likes Pam, you know, and Andy says she's a fine teacher. We're glad you're going to settle here."

"I even bought a business in town, that old two bay self serve car wash off Minter."

"Man, that place has been closed since 1980."

"Yeah, it's like starting from scratch."

"So you need a place to keep a horse? Horses, that's an expensive habit."

"When you marry a rodeo queen it comes with the territory."

"I got a place you want to look at. Climb in," Jim said, motioning to his pickup.

We drove west on 380 another couple of miles, and Jim pulled up to a locked gate on a red dirt road. He left the truck running, went to the gate, unlocked it, and swung it open. He pulled the truck through the gate before locking it behind us.

"This place is nothing fancy," he said. "It's a three bedroom ranch style from the 1970s. The ranch manager lived here back in the day. Sort of marks the end of my ranch, a back entrance off 380. "

We drove on a few miles down the red strip of road before climbing and then dipping into a small valley. At the valley floor was the ranch house and an aging barn surrounded by a hundred acres of fenced-in hard scrabble. The windmill, though ancient, still spun and water overflowed the water trough at its base. I immediately realized that the farm had a lot of prepper potential.

"I think the house could be made habitable without too much trouble," Jim said. "Still has eclectic and well water. Last time I checked, the septic was good. Now I'm not so sure about the barn. I'd give you a good deal on the place and a hundred acres if you would agree to give me a heads up if you see any strangers going down this road. Should be just you, me, and a few ranch hands."

So we made a deal. I financed with one of the two banks in town and opened a personal and business account in the other. I didn't want to get off on the wrong foot with anybody in Throckmorton. Money from the sale of the Jake's house in Ft. Worth would eventually cover more than half of what Jim wanted for the hundred acre farm.

As the wedding date approached and I continued to rebuild the two bay and work on the house and farm, I seemed to drift in and out of reality and dream state.

The dream: Welcome to Greyhound Pride Car Wash. That's what the sign on the roof says. And next to the sign there's a twelve foot long steel greyhound sculpture by Joe Barrington, a sort of greyhound version of the *Bridle Bit* longhorn out on highway 380. The equipment functions flawlessly. The lot is spotless. Out front, a ramada shades the vacs, a fountain, and a couple of picnic tables where we host fund-raising car washes and barbeques for the dreamed of rodeo team.

The reality: Rebuilding the junked two bay turned out to be an expensive mess. I would be lucky to open by Labor Day, and we would probably never make any money.

The dream: The mini ranch is my EMP bug out. Under the floor of the expanded, rebuilt barn is a "storm shelter" full of freeze dried food, canned goods and rice and beans. There is a safe full of silver and gold coins and another safe full of guns. Crates of ammo are stored in the corners. I've buried a thousand gallon propane tank adjacent to the house, and the roof sparkles with solar panels. I've not only insulated the barn so Tex, Pam's horse, and all the other livestock can be secure and warm, but I have also turned the barn into a Faraday cage so my electronic gear and a pickup truck will

152

have protection from the EMP. We have chickens and rabbits and a garden watered by the windmill. We spend much of our time at the ranch house, which I have remolded, fortifying doors and walls against rifle fire. I'm converting one of the bedrooms into a nursery.

The reality: The barn's falling down and the ranch house needs some tender loving care and about thirty thousand dollars worth of repair. We will probably have to live at Pam's house in Throckmorton for at least a semester or two. And odds are that the EMP won't happen anyway.

The dream: I am Chair of the English Department, such as it is, at Cisco Junior College in Cisco, Texas. My recent book on end-of-the-world fiction has been well received. It's an easy commute from Throckmorton to Cisco, and I usually sip an IPA on the way home since the cops rarely ride the back roads.

The reality: I have an appointment for an interview at Cisco Junior College. The Chair of the English Department, a poet (but not a cowboy poet, thank God) named Cletus, thinks there might be an opening for an adjunct who can teach a night class once a week. If I get the appointment, I'll spend all my salary on gas and car repair.

The dream: I'm married to a beautiful Realist rodeo queen who teaches high school English in Throckmorton, Texas.

The reality: Soon I will marry a beautiful Realist former rodeo queen who teaches high school English in Throckmorton, Texas. Last night when we were playing our "quotes" game she paraphrased Kurt Vonnegut: "Marriage is a nation of two," she said. "But we may soon add a colony and be three."

Tomorrow we drive to Perryton, about four and a half hours from Throckmorton, first through the Cap Rock then down onto the flat Panhandle with its wind, dust, and irrigated cotton fields. I'll finally get to meet Pam's parents and Tex, and the wedding is scheduled for the morning of June 30 at the Presbyterian church. After the wedding, Pam and I drive south to Amarillo where we fly to Denver and then Calgary. Honeymoon at the Stampede.

Even though Pam and I have been together for a while now, I know that marriage will be a "voyage on uncharted sea." But I also hope for a "safe haven." And in the event that our "nation of two" becomes a continent of three, or even four, I have decided to keep a written record of our history. I will write in all down, and, in honor of Uncle Jake, I'll call the memoir *Maintaining Greyhound Pride.*